BILL

Life is a game ...

And the ...

Let Modern™ Roma ... jet-set ...
to meet eight n ... ... rs of the world.
From rich tycoons to royal playboys—
they're red-hot and ruthless!

8 volumes in all to collect!

Dear Reader

Welcome to my contribution to *International Billionaires*! Since I come from Wales, where Rugby is not just a game but almost a religion, I was only too delighted to write one of the stories.

Over the years my father, husband and son all played Rugby in the first fifteen at their various schools, and my brother captained his university team, which meant the game was in my blood from early childhood. It was soon the same for my son (who played at fly half), also for my daughter, who is as hotly enthusiastic a fan as her brother. They watch Six Nations matches together, kitted out in the red shirts of Wales and yelling their heads off for the home team. (I do my share of shouting, too.)

As a background to a romantic novel, the game of rugby football provides great heroes: big, muscular men, doing battle like gladiators in a packed arena, with fans cheering them on. So with them in mind the rest soon fell into place.

I hope you enjoy my Rugby story as much as I enjoyed writing it.

Happy reading!

Love

Catherine

THE
ITALIAN COUNT'S
DEFIANT BRIDE

BY
CATHERINE GEORGE

MILLS & BOON®
Pure reading pleasure™

All the characters in this book have no existence outside the imagination of the author, and have no relation whatsoever to anyone bearing the same name or names. They are not even distantly inspired by any individual known or unknown to the author, and all the incidents are pure invention.

First published in Great Britain 2009
Harlequin Mills & Boon Limited,
Eton House, 18-24 Paradise Road, Richmond, Surrey TW9 1SR

© Harlequin Books SA 2009

Special thanks and acknowledgement are given to Catherine George

ISBN: 978 0 263 87211 8

Set in Times Roman 10 on 11 pt
01-0609-57107

Printed and bound in Spain
by Litografia Rosés, S.A., Barcelona

Catherine George was born in Wales, and early on developed a passion for reading which eventually fuelled her compulsion to write. Marriage to an engineer led to nine years in Brazil, but on his later travels the education of her son and daughter kept her in the UK. And, instead of constant reading to pass her lonely evenings, she began to write the first of her romantic novels. When not writing and reading she loves to cook, listen to opera and browse in antiques shops.

Recent titles by this author:

*CHRISTMAS REUNION
THE MILLIONAIRE'S REBELLIOUS MISTRESS
THE MILLIONAIRE'S CONVENIENT BRIDE
THE RICH MAN'S BRIDE

*In the anthology *Married by Christmas*

To rugby players of all nationalities, with a special dedication to the men who wear the red shirts of Wales.

CHAPTER ONE

THE atmosphere in the city was electric. Alicia Cross felt it tingle in her veins as she joined the Welsh rugby fans streaming into Cardiff's Millennium Stadium. As always they had arrived in their thousands to support their heroes, with the added excitement that today a victory against Italy would mean a step forward towards the holy grail of the Six Nations contest, the grand slam; victory over all five of the other teams. Wales were now level with England on wins.

After weeks of travel and hard work to organise parties and press events, Alicia had begged a couple of hours off duty this afternoon to watch the match with friends. Earlier she had checked the arrangements for the sponsor's lunch at the stadium, then hurried back to Cardiff Bay to ensure that all was ready in the hotel chosen for the party later that night. But now at last, instead of joining the sponsors in their hospitality box, she was on her way to her seat in the stands, and she was cutting it a bit fine. In her rush she almost bumped into the man who stepped in front of her, barring her way. She opened her mouth to apologise then snapped it shut, the colour draining from her face. In a knee-jerk reaction she flung away, but he was too quick for her and seized her hand. Conscious of curious glances beamed in their direction, she forced herself to stand still, her heart thudding against her ribs as she looked up into the handsome, unforgettable face of the man who had once changed her girlhood dreams into nightmares.

'Alicia,' he said in the voice that had not, to her intense disgust, lost the power to send shivers down her spine. Eyes locked with hers, he held her hand captive.

She returned the intent, heavy-lidded gaze for the space of several, deliberate heartbeats, then wrenched her hand away and turned on her heel.

But Francesco da Luca caught her by the elbow. 'Alicia, wait. I must speak with you.'

She stared at him in silent disdain, refusal blazing in her eyes as a crowd of late arrivals surged through the turnstiles to jostle them, and with a smothered curse he let her go.

'Do not think you can escape me again so easily, Alicia!'

The hint of menace in the deep, husky voice sent her racing up after the other fans as though the devil were after her. She shot into the cauldron of noise and music in the famous arena, and dived down the steep steps at such breakneck speed that Gareth Davies leapt up from the end of a row to seize her by the arm.

'Steady on, you'll break your neck.'

'Where have you *been*?' demanded Meg indignantly, as her brother thrust Alicia into the seat between them. 'The teams are just about to come on— Hey, what's up?'

'Big rush.' Alicia leaned across to smile at Meg's husband. 'Hi, Rhys.'

'Are you all right, love?' he said, reaching to pat her hand.

'Fine.' Or she would be in a minute.

'You don't look it,' Gareth told her.

Alicia's reply was drowned by the roar from the Italian supporters as their team ran onto the pitch. Then the entire arena erupted as Billy Wales, the famous ram mascot of the Welsh Guards, was led out from the players' tunnel. The big Welsh captain came next, holding a tiny red-shirted boy by the hand as he led his team to line up for the royal presentation.

The smiling prince went along the line, shaking the hands of players on both teams, saying a word here and there. Once he was escorted back to his seat the band of the Welsh Guards struck up the first bars of the Italian national anthem, and the Italian fans in the arena roared out the words to encourage their team. There were cheers as it ended, but a hush fell as the band played the first chords of the Welsh national anthem and every Welsh man, woman and child in the stadium—including those in the home team line-up not too choked with emotion—sang in one voice. Hairs rose on every patriotic neck present as the sound filled the stadium.

The band marched off to cheers, the referee blew the whistle, and from the moment the first ball was lofted to start the match excitement wound the crowd to fever pitch. Alicia cheered and gasped with the others as the tide of play went first one way, then the other. Like everyone else she screamed encouragement when a long pass from the Welsh scrum-half began a running movement which brought the crowd to its feet as Welsh backs surged towards the line, dodging the tackles of their Italian opponents as they passed the ball from hand to hand. The noise from the crowd mounted to a frenzied crescendo when the quicksilver Welsh wing caught the final pass from the full back, danced his way through the chasing Italian defenders and dived over the line to score. Alicia applauded wildly, then after a moment's hush joined in the cheers as the outside half sent the ball sailing over the bar, plum between the posts, to convert the try.

But through it all, even as she hugged Meg in triumph, one part of Alicia's brain was still numb with shock from the confrontation with Francesco da Luca. She had known only too well that he might come here to support his country in such an important match. But in the throes of the Six Nations season there was no way she could have taken time off from her job today purely on the off-chance that he might turn up, even less explain why. None of her colleagues knew about her connection to Francesco.

When the final whistle blew at last to confirm Welsh victory, the crowd went wild. Not a soul in the stadium moved to leave, and the crowd cheered and yelled as the euphoric Welsh squad saluted their supporters.

'How absolutely wonderful! But duty calls. I've got to go now, folks,' said Alicia, getting up. 'You stay here and enjoy the celebration.'

'Are you sure?' said Gareth, torn between seeing her out safely and wallowing in national euphoria.

'Of course. I'll see you at lunch tomorrow.' As Alicia leaned down to kiss Meg, her friend gave her an anxious look.

'I hope you're not too late to bed tonight, Lally. You look tired.'

'I'm fine, Mother Hen. Cheers, boys.'

Alicia made her way up the tiers of wildly cheering fans, returning the jubilant smiles on all sides as she went. But her smile vanished when she spotted the elegant, raincoated figure waiting just outside the exit. For a split second she considered racing back down to the others. Instead she stiffened her spine and mounted the remaining steps, head high. She ignored the hand Francesco held out, but in silent, icy acquiescence accompanied him down to ground level and outside to the entrance of the stadium. As silent as Alicia, he put up a large black umbrella and put an arm round her rigid waist to draw her under its shelter as the first of the exultant Welsh crowd began streaming past them on their way to begin celebrating their team's magnificent victory.

'I must talk with you,' said Francesco at last, dropping his arm as he leaned close to speak in her ear.

'No,' she said flatly.

'I understand your hostility—'

'No one better!'

His eyes blazed. 'You know very well how many, many times I have tried to contact you, Alicia, but you do not return my calls; my letters come back to me unopened. And appeals to your mother have been useless. She would tell me nothing.'

'Of course not. She was acting on my instructions.' Her chin lifted. 'And you can't have appealed to her lately. She moved from Blake Street ages ago.'

He drew her aside to avoid being buffeted by the crowds. 'Dio, this is impossible. Come with me to my hotel.'

She gave him a look like a thrown dagger. 'After what happened last time we were in a hotel room? In your dreams, Francesco!' She tried to thrust his arm away, but he held her fast.

'Dreams of you are all I have!' His eyes locked with hers. 'I felt hope when I finally received a letter from you, but it was merely your—your *condoglianze* for the death of my mother.'

'And you only had that because *my* mother insisted I write it after your letter was forwarded to her.'

His eyes darkened. 'Do you hate me so much then, Alicia?'

She gave him a pitying smile. 'Good heavens, no. I feel nothing at all for you any more, Francesco. This urgent talk you want,' she added briskly, 'I assume it's a divorce you're after? If so you don't need me to agree to it after all this time, unless the law's different in your part of the world. And to set your mind at rest, Signor Conte, I don't want a single thing from you, legally or any other way. So go ahead, get on with it. I'll sign whatever papers you want. As far as I'm concerned you're a free man.'

He shook his head slowly, a look in his eyes she didn't care for at all. 'You and I were married by a priest in the sight of God, Alicia. You are still my wife. And I,' he added, in a tone she cared even less for, 'am still your husband.'

'Only on paper! As a bride I fell disastrously short of your requirements. Something you made cruelly plain to me.' She raised an eyebrow. 'Surely you can just get the marriage annulled?'

'And make public what is personal between us?' He shook his head, and bent nearer under cover of the umbrella. 'After all this time I doubt that you are still a virgin. And if you are not—' he shrugged in the way she remembered only too well '—there is no proof that our marriage was not consummated.'

Alicia's eyes glittered with icy distaste. 'Your problem, not mine, Francesco. I have no plans to marry again. These days I enjoy less binding relationships.' She looked at her watch, then gave him a bored little smile. 'Fascinating though this is, I have to go.'

Francesco released her so abruptly she almost staggered. '*Va bene.* Do what you do so well—run away again, Alicia.'

She tried to think of some crushing response, but in the end just turned on her heel and left him, forcing herself to walk rather than take to her heels as she longed to. She glanced back through the throng to see if Francesco was watching her, but the tall figure in the long black raincoat had vanished. And with it all her pleasure in the day.

Alicia tried hard to blank the encounter from her mind as she got ready for the party that evening. In a routine she'd long since got down to a fine art, she tamed her newly washed hair with a miracle preparation that transformed rebellious curls into glossy obedience, then sleeked them up into a sophisticated knot and went to work on her face. But she functioned like an automaton, her eyes absent, and her disobedient mind full of memories the encounter with Francesco had brought flooding back. Not that they'd ever gone away.

On her eighteenth birthday, blissfully unaware that her life was about to change forever, Alicia had set out to explore Florence alone on the first day of the holiday. With a city map for a guide, she'd threaded her way through ancient streets with fascinating names, and felt very pleased with herself when she eventually reached the Piazza della Signoria. Eyes blazing with excitement behind her dark glasses, she edged her way through the crowds and clustering pigeons to marvel at sights familiar from art books and television, but most of all from a favourite film: *A Room With a View*. Making a mental note of every detail to report back later, she headed at last for the famous Caffe Rivoire. But as she dodged like a rugby fly-half to avoid a pair of kissing lovers, she dropped her bag and lunged after it in such panic only the lightning reflexes of the man she collided with saved her from falling flat on her face as she snatched it up.

'Mi dispiace!' said a voice as hard, safe hands held her steady.

Flushed with embarrassment, Alicia looked up into a striking, honey-skinned face crowned by black curling hair, a face so familiar that every Italian phrase she'd tried to learn vanished from her brain as she stared, dazed, at her rescuer.

'I'm so sorry, it was my fault,' she managed, when she could trust her voice.

Her rescuer smiled. 'Ah! You are English. And you are trembling, *piccola*. Are you hurt?'

'No.' Just knocked sideways by meeting the man whose photograph lived on her bedroom wall.

'But you had the shock, no? Come. You need a cold drink,' he said firmly. 'Allow me to introduce myself. I am Francesco da Luca.'

Was this was really *happening*? She took in a deep breath to steady herself. 'How do you do? My name's Alicia Cross.'

In the shade of an awning at one of Rivoire's outdoor tables, she took off her huge sunglasses and brand-new white cricket hat and smiled shyly as she asked for hot chocolate instead of something cold. 'I was told it's a speciality here. I was on my way to treat myself when I ran into you...' She trailed into silence as she met the arrested look in Francesco da Luca's eyes.

He blinked, murmured an apology, gave the order to a waiter, then leaned back in his chair. 'So. You are in Firenze on holiday, Miss Alicia Cross?'

'Yes.'

He arched a dark eyebrow. 'Alone so young?'

'No.' Just how young did he think she was? 'I'm here with my best friend. Megan was airsick on the flight this morning, so she's sleeping it off at our hotel. But she insisted I come out to explore on my own.' Alicia smiled. 'And gave me a long list of instructions before I left.'

'I can guess one of these.' His answering smile set her pulse racing. 'You must not talk to strangers.'

Twin dimples flickered at the corners of her mouth. 'Top of the list.' Her smile faded as his eyes lit with the unsettling look again. 'Sorry. I didn't mean to offend you.'

'I am not offended—I am charmed by the *fossetti*,' he said softly.

The word hadn't come up in Alicia's phrase book, but she was pretty sure he meant her freckles. 'I hate them,' she said passionately, then smiled as the waiter set her chocolate in front of her and thanked him with the one word of Italian she could remember.

Francesco leaned nearer. 'You should not hate them,' he informed her. 'They are enchanting.'

Alicia sipped some of her chocolate. 'Not to me,' she said, resigned. 'I've tried all sorts of things to get rid of them, but nothing works.'

He frowned. 'I think we have a language problem. Smile again for me, *per favore*.'

Alicia obeyed, her smile widening as she realised he meant her dimples. Not that she was hugely keen on those, either. She brushed a finger over her cheekbones. 'I thought you meant the freckles.'

'They also are charming,' he informed her gravely.

Not sure how to answer that, Alicia took refuge in her chocolate, which went down like liquid gold as she marvelled at her wonderful luck. She was here at last in Florence, with all the world going by in the afternoon sun in this famous *piazza* full of statues and wonderful architecture. And to top that she was actually, unbelievably, doing all this in the company of Francesco da Luca.

'What are you thinking?' he asked at last.

'That you speak very good English, Signor da Luca.' With a slight accent that sent shivers down her spine.

'*Grazie*, but I am Francesco, please. And I speak English,' he added, 'because it is a great advantage in my business.'

His sporting career had been so brief Alicia had never discovered anything about his private life. 'What do you do?' She flushed. 'I'm sorry. You don't have to answer that.'

Francesco shook his head, amused. 'What man does not like to talk about himself?'

Alicia beamed. As far as she was concerned he could talk about himself as long as he liked.

Francesco sat back in his seat, apparently happy to oblige her.

'I studied law, but although the knowledge I gained is useful to me I do not practise it.' He shrugged his broad shoulders. 'For me life is wine, olives and marble. And responsibilities.' He shot her a searching look. 'And you, Miss Alicia; you are still in school?'

'No. Though I was until last week,' she added honestly. 'I've just finished my exams. If my grades are good enough, I go on to university in October.'

'Then you are not as young as I thought,' he said, surprised, and leaned forward again. 'So. How old are you, Alicia?'

'Eighteen.' She hesitated, then smiled, for once deliberately bringing her dimples into full play. 'Today, in fact.'

His heavy-lidded eyes opened wide and her heart skipped a beat as she saw they were a translucent shade somewhere between green and blue; improbable and unexpected in such a masculine face.

'It is your birthday!' Francesco exclaimed. *'Buon compleanno!'*

'Thank you.'

'But instead of chocolate to celebrate you should have champagne, or a glass of our own prosecco. Now you are a grown-up lady this is allowed, no?'

She smiled. 'Will you laugh if I say I'm not very keen on champagne?'

'No,' he said very softly. 'I will not laugh.'

Silence fell between them as the spectacular eyes held hers. Alicia gazed at him, mesmerised, then blinked at last and braced herself to confess 'Actually, I know who you are.'

He nodded, smiling. 'Because I told you my name.'

'No. I mean that I once saw you play rugby.'

'Davverro?' he exclaimed, astonished.

She nodded and named the tournament in which she'd seen him play.

'Few people remember that! I was injured soon afterwards and never played at that level again.' Francesco shook his head in wonder. 'You were just a child—also a girl. I am amazed.'

'That I remember you, or that I'm a girl who likes rugby?'

'Both of these. Your father played?'

'I don't know. I've never met him,' she said, and could have bitten her tongue the moment the words were out.

Francesco winced. *'Mi dispiace!'*

She tried to make her shrug nonchalant. 'I follow the game because my best friend's father is a rugby fanatic, her brother too. I used to watch Gareth's school matches with Meg, then his club matches later on. Once he even got us tickets for an international at the Millennium Stadium in Cardiff.'

'An impressive arena,' he agreed. 'I have been there to watch Italy play against Wales.'

'Do you miss playing rugby?'

'Yes.' He shrugged impressive shoulders. 'But I have no time for sport in my life now, except to watch on television. Will such an ardent rugby-fan look at me in disgust if I confess I also follow Fiorentino, the local soccer-team here?'

Alicia shook her head, smiling. Then she glanced at her watch and saw that they'd been sitting there far longer than she'd thought. With a sigh she replaced her dark glasses and pulled her hat down low over them. 'It's time I got back to my friend. Thank you for the chocolate—and for being so kind.'

Francesco rose quickly. 'Where are you staying?'

She gave him the name of a small hotel in a quiet residential area well away from the town centre. 'It was recommended by one of my mother's friends.'

'Bene. I shall escort you back.' He bent his head to smile under the green-lined brim of her hat as they left the table. 'I must make sure you return to your friend safely on your special day, Miss Alicia Cross.'

On her own earlier the route to the Piazza della Signoria had seemed quite long while she was finding her way, but the walk back with Francesco was far too short for Alicia, as she talked about her plans for the holiday as though she'd known him for years. Which in one way she had. When they arrived at the hotel she held out her hand.

'Thank you again. It was an amazing coincidence to meet you.' She smiled shyly. 'And such a pleasure.'

To her delight Francesco kissed her hand. 'It was a great pleasure for me also, Miss Alicia Cross. I hope you find your friend recovered. *Arrivederci.*'

Alicia went up in the lift in a daze, gazing at the back of her hand as though Francesco's kiss was engraved on it. She came back to earth as the doors opened and hurried to knock on the door of their room, calling softly, 'Sorry to get you out of bed. It's me.'

Megan Davies blinked owlishly when she finally opened the door. 'You're back soon. I thought you'd be ages yet.'

'I was worried about you.' Alicia eyed her critically. 'How do you feel?'

'Feeble, but not throwing up any more. I'll be fine tomorrow.' Meg sighed despondently. 'Which isn't much use. Your birthday's today.'

'We'll celebrate it tomorrow. In the meantime, lie down again; you still look peaky.' Alicia plumped her friend's pillows up invitingly.

'So come on then, Lally,' demanded Meg as she subsided against them. 'Tell me what you've seen!'

'I found the Piazza della Signoria quite easily. It's not far, and just as amazing as expected, like a great outdoor sculpture-gallery. I had a look at the Palazzo Vecchio, though I didn't go inside, then I went past the crowds round the Neptune fountain to look at the replica of David and the statues in the Loggia dei Lanzi. The Rape of the Sabines is pretty realistic,' added Alicia with relish. 'But my favourite is Perseus holding the severed head of Medusa.'

'Can't wait! Did you splurge on a birthday hot chocolate at Rivoire afterwards?'

'Sort of, yes.'

'What do you mean, "sort of"?'

Alicia took in a deep breath, her eyes blazing with excitement. 'You'll never guess who I ran into.'

Megan's eyes widened. 'The minute you're let loose in Florence? Who?'

With drama, Alicia described the incident with her bag and the man who came to her rescue.

Meg snorted. 'You mean that after all my dire warnings you let someone pick you up?'

'Yes, Mother Hen! Literally. Otherwise I would have fallen on my nose.'

'This rescuer—was he Italian?'

'What did you expect, someone from Cardiff?' Alicia's dimples flashed wickedly. 'Are you sitting comfortably, Megan dear? Because here's the bit you won't believe. It was Francesco da Luca.'

Meg stared at her, open-mouthed. 'The Italian winger from your rugby gallery?'

'The man himself.' Alicia laid a hand on her heart. 'The object of my girlish adoration.'

'Did you tell him that?'

'Of *course* not. But I did say I was a rugby fan.'

'So what happened then?'

'He insisted on buying me a cold drink to get over my little shock—only I asked for chocolate—and we sat at one of the outside Rivoire tables. We talked for ages, then he walked back here with me.' Alicia smiled rapturously. 'It must have been fate that sent me tumbling in front of him.'

'And kindly made me sick so you were on your own,' said Meg darkly, then grinned. 'But I'm glad you had some excitement on your birthday, love.'

'My mother will never believe me!'

'Nor mine!' Meg yawned widely. 'Look, I'm not up to eating yet, but you must be hungry.'

'Not really, after the hot chocolate. And you still look tired, so get your head down again. I'll read for a while outside on the terrace.' Alicia waved a paperback with anticipation. 'What a treat! Fiction to wallow in instead of endless text-books. Try to sleep. I'll see you later.'

But when she finally settled under an umbrella Alicia was too wired to concentrate on her novel. Instead she leaned back, eyes closed, reliving every moment of the meeting with Francesco. Eventually she gave up even pretending to read and went inside to see if Meg felt like eating something.

'Great—I was just about to text you! Those just arrived.' Meg yanked Alicia into the room to show her the flowers on the dressing table. 'The receptionist brought them up. The posy of carnations is for me, because the card wishes me a swift recovery, but the roses are for Miss Alicia Cross.'

Alicia gazed in delight at the creamy, half-open blooms. The message on the card wished her a happy birthday, and asked Miss Alicia Cross and her friend to give Francesco da Luca the pleasure of dining with him that evening. He would call for them at eight to see if this was agreeable.

'Agreeable? It's fantastic! Sorry I was nosy, but I just had to see what he said.' Meg's eyes glittered in her pallid face. 'So get your party dress on, girl. This is your night!'

'It most certainly is not! I'm not leaving you on your own again, Megan,' said Alicia indignantly. 'When Francesco comes I'll tell him you're not well enough, and thank him nicely and say maybe some other time.'

'Are you *nuts*? There won't be another time.' Meg pulled Alicia down on the edge of the bed beside her. 'Look, this is a one-off, Lally. Go for it. If you're in doubt ring your mother again first and see what she says.'

Alicia grinned ruefully. 'If I do that, Bron will say no.'

'And you really want to go out with your Francesco?'

'Of course I do. But I wish you were well enough to go too.'

'So do I, but as I look totally gruesome and can't face the thought of food it's just not on. Give Francesco my regrets.' Meg patted Alicia's hand. 'Ring down for some tea for me, then hit the shower, deck yourself in some of your birthday gear, and get ready to party!'

There was soon a lot more argument while Alicia hassled the

invalid into eating some of the toast ordered with the tea. But in the end she gave in to Meg's urging and began to get ready.

'Bron insisted I pack the dress she bought as part of my present, so do you think I'd better wear it tonight?' Alicia asked, holding it against her.

'Of course! That coffee-cream shade looks good on you. Subtle but pretty.'

'I wanted black and strapless, not pretty,' sighed Alicia. 'But Bron vetoed that.' She shivered suddenly and hung the dress back in the wardrobe. 'Look, I'm not sure this evening's a good idea—I'll stay here with you.'

'Rubbish. If you don't keep your date with Signor Dreamboat, you'll never stop kicking yourself afterwards. Now, move. Get into the underwear I gave you, and I'll lend a hand with your hair after you do your face.'

All her life Alicia had longed for straight, dark hair like Meg's. To tame her curly, coppery mane she usually wove it into a thick braid, but because this was a one-off special occasion Meg insisted on wielding the hair dryer and created looser waves that she ordered Alicia to leave down for once.

'Looks great like that. Now, put your frock on and I'll fall in a heap while you add the finishing touches.' She crawled back into bed with a sigh of relief.

'Oh Meg!' said Alicia in remorse. 'Now look at you.'

'I'm fine. Hurry up. Put the new heels on and give me a twirl.'

Alicia pulled a face as she obeyed. 'I hope I don't have to walk far in these.' She transferred a few belongings to a small clutch-bag and fastened on the gold chain-bracelet Meg's parents had given her. 'Are you sure you'll be all right? I've got my posh new phone if you need me.'

'I won't need you. I'll read or watch telly.' Meg smiled encouragingly. 'For heaven's sake go, girl. Enjoy your birthday!'

But Alicia suffered a bad attack of cold feet as she went down in the lift. Francesco might get entirely the wrong idea when she turned up alone. He knew nothing about her or her background.

He might think she did this kind of thing all the time, whereas Meg's brother Gareth and his friends were the only boys she knew. And to them she was just a freckle-faced kid.

When she reached the foyer Alicia's heart leapt as Francesco walked through the door. Elegant in a superb linen suit, he was so much her every dream come true she pinched herself surreptitiously to make sure this was really happening.

'*Buona sera,*' he said, taking her hand. 'You look delightful, Miss Alicia Cross.'

'Thank you.' She smiled shyly. 'Meg and I both thank you very much for the flowers, too, but I'm afraid there's a problem—'

'You cannot dine with me?' he said quickly, his smile fading.

'Meg's not well enough to come.' Alicia eyed him uncertainly. 'Is it all right if I come with you on my own?'

Francesco's eyes lit with a look which set her pulse racing. 'It is perfect. I am most honoured to help you celebrate your birthday.' He took a phone from his pocket. 'I will ring the restaurant.' After a short, rapid-fire conversation he led Alicia outside into the balmy, starlit night. 'We are dining in Santa Croce. Can you walk that far in those shoes?'

She nodded fervently. Even if she had blisters tomorrow.

Florence after dark was so vibrant with noise and life, and the constant background noise of traffic and inevitable motor scooters. Alicia took in a deep, relishing breath, drinking it in like nectar as Francesco led her through the still-crowded Piazza della Signoria where at outside tables couples were drinking cocktails and people-watching in the balmy evening. Neptune loomed in his fountain, sleek and silvery-pale in the floodlights with his attendant water-nymphs, but Alicia's eyes went straight to the Loggia dei Lanzi where Perseus held his gruesome trophy aloft.

'You like that statue?' asked Francesco, watching, and she nodded happily.

'But I love everything here. I've looked forward to the holiday for so long, I was afraid I might be disappointed.' She smiled up at him. 'But your city is even more wonderful than I'd imagined.'

'It is beautiful,' he agreed as they left the *piazza* behind to make for Santa Croce. 'But it is not *my* city. I am here for a few days on business. I do not live here. My home is in Montedaluca.'

As they passed the floodlit façade of the great Santa Croce church, it suddenly struck Alicia that in the town that had his name in it he might well have a wife and family. Something she should have checked on long before now.

Francesco came to a halt soon afterwards outside the ancient *palazzo* which housed the restaurant. 'Something worries you,' he said in the slow, careful English which had surprised her from the first. She would have expected an Italian to talk quickly, with a lot of hand waving. But there was an inner stillness to Francesco da Luca she found deeply fascinating. 'What troubles you, Alicia?'

She braced herself. 'Are you married?'

'Ah, I see! What would you do if I say yes?' he asked, amused, sending her heart plummeting down to the new shoes.

'Go straight back to the hotel,' she said promptly. And cry into her pillow.

'Without your birthday dinner?' He smiled. 'Then it is a good thing, *cara*, that I am not married.' He threw out a hand. 'No wife, no *fidanzata*.'

'What's that?'

'A fiancée, Miss Alicia.' He looked suddenly stern. 'If I had possessed either I would not have requested your company tonight.'

Her chin lifted defiantly. 'I had to ask.'

'*Naturalmente.*' He smiled and took her hand. 'Now, let us eat.'

An elegant woman at the reception desk led them through the crowded restaurant to a small group of tables for two on a raised dais at the back of the room. Alicia gazed at her surroundings in delight as Francesco held her chair for her. Faded haughty faces of mediaeval knights looked down on them from frescoed walls, their rearing horses and lean hunting-dogs given the illusion of movement by the flickering candles on the tables. Alicia was suddenly grateful for her mother's faultless taste. Her simple little sheath-dress, for all its simplicity—or because of it—felt exactly right here. As Francesco held her chair for her Alicia's eyes widened. On her plate lay a single, creamy rose. She gazed up at him in delight as she thanked him, thinking how aristocratic he looked, so very obviously at home in surroundings like this.

'I chose it with care,' he informed her, his eyes gleaming in the candlelight. 'See? The petals are the colour and velvet texture of your skin.'

Thankful that due to this same texture her skin rarely showed blushes, she smiled at him luminously. 'Thank you for making my birthday so special for me.'

'It is my great pleasure,' Francesco assured her as a waiter filled their glasses. '*Allora*, even if you do not care for it you must have one sip of champagne to celebrate this special day. Happy birthday, Alicia.'

She smiled as he raised his glass in a toast and touched it with her own, and to please him drank a little. And found that this champagne was pure nectar. 'It's delicious,' she told him, surprised.

He smiled indulgently. 'I am glad it pleases you. Now, tell me what you like to eat.'

Alicia took one look at the daunting menu and appealed to Francesco. 'Will you help me choose?'

His eyes gleamed bright in the candlelight as they smiled into hers. 'I will do anything you wish, *cara*.'

Afterwards Alicia had very little recollection of the delicious *antipasti* she was served, or the meltingly tender lamb with artichokes that followed. She was so enchanted with Francesco and Florence that the food was of secondary importance as they talked together in a little candlelit oasis of privacy on their dais above the other diners in the crowded restaurant.

'So where did you go to school, Alicia?' he asked.

'In a convent,' she admitted reluctantly. 'When the nuns heard we were coming to Florence, they told us we must visit Santa Croce—but they meant the church, not a restaurant like this.'

'You are a Catholic?'

'Yes. Are you?'

He nodded. 'But not as devout as my mother would wish.'

'I'm not as devout as Bron, either.'

'Bron?'

'My mother, Bronwen Cross. As I mentioned before, I've never met my biological father,' she said matter-of-factly. 'Is your father still alive?'

His eyes shadowed. 'No. My parents married late. He died when I was young.'

'I'm so sorry.' She touched his hand in sympathy. 'Brothers, sisters?'

'None.'

'So your mother just has you.'

'*Davvero*,' he said heavily, then smiled and changed the subject. 'I would offer you more champagne, but perhaps it is better you keep to one glass.'

'Much better,' she agreed, and with a sigh glanced at her watch. 'The entire evening has been so lovely, Francesco, but now I must get back to Meg.'

As they left the restaurant Alicia stumbled a little in her new heels, and Francesco took her hand to steady her, then kept it in his to walk back to the hotel. For Alicia the warm, hard clasp of Francesco's hand in hers was the crowning touch of the entire evening. As they neared the hotel he drew her to a halt in the shadows in the quiet street.

'Tomorrow I have business matters to attend to during the day, but in the evening will you dine with me again, Alicia? Your friend also, if she is well enough.' He smiled into her startled eyes. 'Say yes.'

'I need to ask Meg first,' she hedged, secretly ecstatic.

'Do you have a *telefonino*—a mobile phone?'

She nodded. 'Megan's brother gave me a new one for my birthday.'

'Give it to me, then. I will enter my number into it, and yours into mine. *Allora*,' Francesco said with satisfaction when he'd finished, 'we can communicate.' He paused and moved closer.

'Though there are other ways to communicate, Alicia—the most delightful way is a kiss to wish you happy birthday.' He drew her very gently into his arms in the shadows. 'Passers by will not think it remarkable to see people kissing.'

Alicia stood very still in his embrace, her heart hammering. She had been hoping, longing, for Francesco da Luca to kiss her. She had dreamed about it often enough in the past when his photograph was the last thing she saw before going to sleep every night.

Francesco bent his head, his lips gentle at first. But at the first touch of them against hers she responded so helplessly she felt his athlete's body tense against her. His arms tightened as her lips parted, his tongue found hers in a caress that took her breath away, and the kiss quickly grew so urgent Alicia's head reeled when his arms finally fell away.

He stood back, breathing hard as he stared down at her blankly. *'Mi dispiace,'* he said hoarsely. 'I did not expect…'

'Neither did I,' she said with feeling, and took in a deep breath. 'I've never been kissed like that before.'

He smiled in open male triumph and kissed her again. 'You enchant me, Alicia Cross. I will call for you tomorrow evening.'

'I haven't agreed to that,' she protested.

'Then agree now, *tesoro.*' His eyes locked with hers. 'Say "yes, Francesco, I will be very pleased to dine again with you".'

Instead of saying yes to dinner—and to anything else he wanted—Alicia hung on to every scrap of willpower she possessed. 'Ring me tomorrow and I'll let you know if Meg agrees.'

Francesco tucked an errant curl behind her ear. *'Va bene,* Miss Alicia Cross.' He took her hand and escorted her into the lobby of the hotel. *'A domani,'* he said formally, and waited until the lift doors closed behind her.

CHAPTER TWO

FRANCESCO rang early next morning, before Alicia even had time to worry whether he would or not.

'Whatever he suggests tell him yes!' Meg ordered, as she devoured her breakfast.

'*Buon giorno*, Alicia,' said Francesco. 'How are you today?'

'Good morning. I'm just fine. How are you?'

'Waiting in great suspense,' he said, with a caressing note in his voice. 'Is your friend better?'

'Fighting fit now,' said Alicia, grinning as she pushed the last roll towards Meg.

'*Eccelente*. Please give her my good wishes. So—you will both dine with me this evening?'

'Thank you, we'd love to,' said Alicia, rolling her eyes as Meg punched the air in triumph.

'*Bene*. What will you do today?'

'The usual tourist things.'

'Do not tire yourself with too many such things, *cara*. I shall call for you at eight. *Ciao*.'

'*Ciao*,' she echoed and switched off the phone. 'There, Megan Davies. We've got a date. Satisfied?'

'You could have asked him to bring a friend.'

'You don't want much, do you? Hard luck; you'll just have to share Francesco with me.'

'Playing gooseberry's not my thing, you know,' said Meg ruefully.

'It's not applicable,' said Alicia, blocking out last night's kiss. 'Francesco is just a very kind man taking pity on a couple of convent schoolgirls let loose in Florence for the first time.'

'You *told* him about the convent?' said Meg in disgust, then grinned wickedly. 'I hope you said we just went to school there! Nuns we are not.'

'I might as well be,' said Alicia gloomily. 'I've never had a boyfriend.'

'Only because you're picky—and Rhys Evans was already taken.'

'Bowled over by you the first time Gareth brought him home to supper!' Alicia laughed and hugged her friend. 'Thank goodness you're feeling better. Come on, we're wasting time.'

'Put loads of sunscreen on first—and don't forget your hat and glasses.'

'Yes, Mummy!'

For the rest of the holiday the girls packed in as many sights as possible during the day. In deference to the nuns, they inspected the tombs of Michelangelo and Galileo in the great church of Santa Croce, visited the vast Duomo to marvel at Brunelleschi's dome, then after waiting in line marvelled even more at Michelangelo's mighty David in the Accademia. They queued for hours longer to look at the paintings in the Uffizi, and after wriggling their way to the front of the crowd to look at it close up decided they liked Botticelli's Primavera best. They bought paninis stuffed with ham before visiting the Pitti Palace to look at more paintings, then picnicked afterwards in the Boboli Gardens.

In the narrow streets of Oltrarno—literally the 'other side' of the River Arno—they peered into little workshops where craftsmen carved wood for mirrors and picture frames, or created elegant handbags and gloves from softest leather. They gazed in the jewellers' shops on the Ponte Vecchio, and at designer clothes in the Via Tuornabuoni, fantasising over what they would buy if they had the money. But eventually it was agreed that their favourite place of all was the Bargello, once a prison, now a sculpture museum where Meg fell madly in love with Donatello's nude bronze of David.

'He looks so cute in just his jaunty hat and boots!'

'Only you could call a fabulous work of art *cute*,' said Alicia, laughing.

Each evening Francesco called for them to take them out to dinner and listen to their report on their day, and from the moment Meg first met him she had no more qualms about playing gooseberry. As she told Alicia later, he was as good looking and charming as she'd expected, but his manners were so perfect he made her feel like an asset to the evening instead of an unwanted third.

Both girls had made it plain to Francesco, the moment he arrived the first evening to take them both out, that they must be allowed to pay for their share of the meal. And to Alicia's relief he'd taken them to a lively, packed *trattoria*, very different from the restaurant of the night before, and a great deal less expensive. Meg had loved everything about it, and tucked into her prawn-stuffed ravioli with unashamed gusto after her fast of the previous day. The only flaw in the evening came later when Francesco had insisted on paying the bill after all. But Meg had calculated the cost of their meals to the last euro, and the moment the three of them left the trattoria she presented Francesco with two thirds of the bill in notes.

'Our share,' said Meg firmly, and in the end, under protest, he had to accept.

'But this once only,' he said at last when they refused to budge. '*Allora*, tell me what you have planned for tomorrow.'

When they'd got back to the hotel Meg announced that it was time for her nightly phone call to her boyfriend, and after thanks to Francesco for a fabulous evening she hurried inside and left them together.

'Your friend is not only charming, but tactful,' he said, looking down at Alicia. 'This boyfriend is waiting for her at home?'

'Yes.' She smiled affectionately. 'Rhys thinks Meg hung the moon.'

'He is a man of perception. She is very attractive—not just her looks, but her personality.' Francesco's hand caught hers. 'Do you have a boyfriend waiting for you, Alicia?'

Wishing she could say there were several all counting the minutes until she got back, she shook her head. 'No, I don't.'

'*Ottimo!*' He kissed her hand, then drew her into his arms and kissed her willing mouth. 'I will call for you both at eight tomorrow. And this time I will pay, so no more *argomento*!'

The dream holiday went by so fast the last day arrived all too soon. During a final shopping trip for gifts to take home, Alicia found it hard to be cheerful as they searched for bargains in San Lorenzo, because later that night she would have to say goodbye to Francesco. Once Megan left them outside the hotel after dinner, their few moments alone together would be the last time she would ever see him. And she couldn't bear the thought of it.

Meg eyed her downcast face as they carried their modest haul up to their hotel room, then told her to ring Francesco. 'Ask him if we can eat earlier tonight.'

Alicia eyed her suspiciously as she unlocked their door. 'Why?'

'When Francesco walks us back after dinner, I'll plead packing and phone calls to my mother and Rhys and you two can enjoy an hour alone together. Don't argue. Do it.'

Alicia looked at her friend's vivid face in silence for a moment, then threw her arms round her and hugged her. 'Thank you.'

Meg hugged her back. 'You've done it for me and Rhys often enough, now it's my turn.'

'It's hardly the same thing!'

'It's exactly the same thing. Go on. Ring him.'

When the unmistakeable voice said *'Pronto,'* Alicia took in a deep breath.

'It's me. Alicia.'

'Que cosa? Is something wrong?' Francesco demanded sharply.

'No. Nothing. It's just that Meg—I mean we—well, we wondered if we could have dinner earlier tonight? Because we've got packing and so on.'

'But of course,' he said, with such audible relief Alicia smiled radiantly at Meg. 'I will come for you at seven.'

'Grazie, Francesco. *Ciao.'*

Meg grinned like a Cheshire cat as Alicia switched off her phone. 'Quite the little linguist these days! So, early is good?' Her eyes sparkled. 'Better than Francesco knows. He's such a star, never giving the slightest sign that I'm in the way, but he's obviously desperate to spend time alone with you.'

'No more desperate than I am,' said Alicia, with heat that brought a startled look from Meg. 'Well, it's true. For years I was in love with a photograph, but Francesco in the flesh is a dream come true.'

'Emotive word, "flesh",' said Meg uneasily. 'Until now you've never shown the slightest interest in any man—unless he was covered in mud on a rugby pitch.'

'So isn't it about time I did?' Alicia sucked in a deep breath. 'Oh Meg—I'm so in love with Francesco.'

'I know you are! It's frightening.'

'You feel the same about Rhys!'

'That's different.'

'Why?'

'You've only just met Francesco.'

'I feel as if I've known him forever. Maybe I knew him in another life.'

'You're beginning to worry me, Lally.'

Alicia's wistful smile brought a lump to her friend's throat. 'No need. We've had a wonderful holiday in Florence, and Francesco was part of it; an experience I can look back on and dream about.' Her mouth drooped. 'But it's going to be so hard to say goodbye tonight.'

'I know. That's why I'm giving you time to yourselves.' Meg wagged a stern finger. 'Just make sure you're in by midnight, Cinders.'

When the three of them walked back to the hotel after their early dinner that evening, Megan gave Francesco a beaming smile. 'As a small return for the meals you've paid for, and the restaurants we'd never have discovered on our own, I'm giving you a goodbye present.'

He eyed her in surprise. 'But I need no present, *cara*. I have enjoyed your company very much.'

'I know that. Otherwise I wouldn't have enjoyed myself so much. But now I'm going up to our room on my own to pack and make my phone calls, so you can have Alicia to yourself for an hour or so as a parting gift.'

Francesco leaned down and kissed her on both cheeks. 'You are a very kind lady. This is also your wish?' he demanded, turning to Alicia, and gave her a smile that turned her heart over when she nodded in eager consent. 'Then it is a present I accept with gratitude, Miss Megan Davies. *Mille grazie*.'

When they'd seen Megan inside the hotel Francesco took Alicia's hand to walk back to the Piazza della Signoria. 'I am going to make a request,' he said, oddly sombre. 'You must say no if you do not wish to grant it, *tesoro*.'

By this time finding it hard to imagine saying no to Francesco, no matter what he wanted, Alicia looked up at him expectantly. 'You'll have to tell me what the request is first.'

'You have not asked where I am staying.'

'I took it for granted you were at one of the grander hotels.'

He shook his head. 'I keep an apartment here in Firenze.'

'For your business trips?'

Francesco's quiet laugh was mirthless. 'Officially, yes. But it is also my *rifugio*, my sanctuary, where I can relax alone occasionally away from the demands of my life in Montedaluca. My intention was to spend only two days here this time. But then, Miss Alicia Cross, I met you. And could not leave until you do.'

A statement which sent Alicia's pulse into overdrive. She gazed up at him, starry-eyed. 'This request, Francesco—are you asking me to have coffee in your apartment?'

His smile was answer enough. 'Yes, *carina*. Will you?'

'Of course I will,' she said impatiently. 'Do we have to walk far?'

'No.' To Alicia's surprise he led her to a building in the *piazza* itself, and took her up to the top floor in a lift. '*Allora,*' he said as he unlocked a door. 'Welcome to my *rifugio*.'

The apartment was impressive, with a high, raftered ceiling. But instead of the antiques Alicia had expected the comfortable furniture was contemporary, and the colourful paintings on the walls were abstracts.

'This is so lovely, Francesco,' she said, impressed. 'You could make a fortune letting it out to visitors.'

'There are other apartments in the building for that,' he informed her. 'This one I keep only for myself.'

Alicia's eyes rounded. 'You own the building?'

'It was part of my mother's dowry when she married my father. But she uses it only when she comes to Florence to buy clothes. The responsibility for running it as a commercial enterprise is mine.' He shrugged. 'But I do this willingly, because it gives me an excuse to escape here sometimes to my—what do you say in English?—bolt hole?'

She smiled crookedly. 'A very smart bolt-hole.'

'But I have not shown you the best part,' he said, and put his arm round her.

Sure he meant to rush her off to a bedroom, Alicia wasn't sure whether she was relieved or disappointed when he led her to a window and threw back the shutters. Then she gave such a raucous, boyish whistle he hugged her close, laughing.

She beamed at him in rapture. 'A room with a view, Francesco! And what a view.'

They were opposite the Palazzo Vecchio, with a perfect view of the Loggia dei Lanzi and most of the Piazza della Signoria.

'You may gaze on Perseus from here as much as you like,' he said softly, and cleared his throat. 'I shall make coffee.'

She shook her head. 'In the time we've got left, can't we just sit and talk?'

He took off his jacket and led her to one of the sofas. '*D'accordo*. Some talk is necessary.' He hesitated for a moment, then put his arm round her, and she leaned against him, so pliant and trusting he gave a husky little laugh. 'So innocent, so sweet.'

She turned her head up to give him a wry look. 'I may have gone to school in a convent, Francesco, but I didn't take vows!'

'For which I am passionately grateful,' he said, and kissed her.

And this time, knowing she'd never see him again, Alicia responded with fire fuelled by despair. With a groan Francesco drew her onto his lap, and she caught her breath, thrilled to feel his heart hammering against her. Elated by the effect she was having on him, she returned his kisses with mounting fervour as she breathed in the heady scent of aroused male mingled with something she identified as Aqua di Parma cologne.

At last Francesco tore his mouth away and turned her face into his shoulder, his hand unsteady as he held her head hard against him. '*Tesoro*, forgive me.'

'For what?' she whispered, and pulled away to look up into the tense, handsome face. 'I wanted you to kiss me.'

'I know.'

'How could you tell?' she said, frowning.

He smiled ruefully. 'You made it very plain, *carina*. But,' he added, sobering, 'if you kiss a man like that it is dangerous; he will want more.'

Alicia eyed him with interest. 'Do you?'

'Yes,' he said starkly. 'But I will not take it.'

'Why not?'

He smoothed an unsteady hand over her hair. 'For many

reasons. You are young, and in a country foreign to you—and you are a virgin, no?'

She rolled her eyes. 'I'm a virgin, yes.'

'You are making fun of me!'

'No, I'm not.' As she wriggled closer he caught his breath, and she felt his erection harden against her thighs through the thin fabric of her dress. Now what? she thought in panic. Should she stay where she was and pretend to ignore it, or should she slide tactfully from his lap and say it was time to go? But it wasn't time yet, and she didn't want to go. She quite desperately wanted him to make love to her, for him to be her first lover, even if this was the last time she'd ever see him. 'Francesco,' she whispered, and looked up into eyes which blazed as they met the invitation in hers.

To her dismay he jumped up and set her on her feet. '*Carissima*, you must not look at me like that.' He gestured towards the window. 'I am not marble, like the statues out there. I am flesh and blood, and you know well that I desire you.' He gave a wry laugh and held her close. 'When Megan gave us this last time together, I told myself I would be content just to talk to you for a while. But I am human, and a man—'

'And I'm a woman, Francesco,' whispered Alicia against his chest. 'Make love to me. *Please!*'

'*Dio!*' he exclaimed in anguish. 'You must not say this.'

'Why not?'

'You know well why not,' he said fiercely, his accent more pronounced as he spoke rapidly into her hair. 'I want you. You know this because a man cannot hide his desire. But I have wanted you from that first moment out there below, at the Rivoire. When you took off your hat and sunglasses I looked into those great, dark eyes and felt such an urge to kiss you I was— how do you say?—spellbound.'

Alicia moved away slightly to look up at him, her eyes alight with pure joy at his confession. 'I thought you were put off by my freckles.'

Francesco's eyes softened as he stroked a finger across her

cheekbones. 'I adore your freckles. I adore *you*, Alicia, so much that although I desire it desperately I will not take this precious gift you offer me. At least,' he said, in a tone which made her tremble, 'not tonight.'

'But I'm going home tomorrow,' she said forlornly.

He led her to the sofa again. 'So let us sit down and enjoy this last time for a while together.'

'For a while?'

Francesco took her hand. 'I must go home to Montedaluca first, but very soon I will fly to visit you in your home.'

Alicia's eyes widened to dark saucers as she stared at him. 'Are you serious?'

'You do not wish me to come?' he demanded.

'You know I do!' She swallowed hard. 'I just never imagined in my wildest dreams that I'd see you again once I left.'

'Ah, *carina*,' he said caressingly, and kissed her fingers one by one. 'I told you I wanted you from that first moment. Did you feel the same for me?'

'Oh yes.' She dimpled at him so mischievously he caught his breath, so obviously wanting to kiss her that she touched a hand to his cheek. 'So I think it's time I told you a little story, Francesco da Luca.'

He kissed her nose and sat back, holding her hand. 'Talk then, *diletta mia*.'

'Once upon a time a girl found a picture in a rugby magazine, with a feature and a shot of a Treviso winger scoring a spectacular try. The girl was so impressed she cut the picture out and added it to the gallery of Welsh rugby stars on her bedroom wall.'

Francesco looked down at her in astonishment. 'This is true?'

'We convent-educated girls don't tell lies,' she said sternly, and smiled up at him. 'Every night since then your face has been the last thing I see before going to sleep. I couldn't believe my eyes when I bumped into you out there in the *piazza*.'

'*Un miraculo!*' He kissed her swiftly. 'I was too restless to concentrate on paperwork that afternoon, and suddenly felt a great need to be part of life out there. Fate sent me to catch you when you fell.' Francesco put a finger under her chin. 'And I will never let you go. *Ti amo*, Alicia Cross. Must I translate?'

She shook her head, smiling radiantly. 'I love you too, Francesco da Luca.'

His answering smile took her breath away. 'Do you love me enough to live with me in Montedaluca one day as my wife?'

'Yes,' she said without hesitation.

This time his kiss was not gentle, and she responded to it with joy, then trembled as his hands caressed her through the thin fabric of her dress.

He buried his face in her hair. 'I want you so much.'

She pulled his mouth down to hers. 'Make love to me, Francesco. *Now*. But you'll have to teach me what to do.'

He gave a stifled groan and crushed her to him. 'I will take much, much pleasure in teaching you the art of love, *tesoro*, but not until our wedding night.'

'Why not now?'

'Because I want our first time together to be perfect, with all the time in the world to love each other.' He smoothed the tumbled curls back from her forehead. 'I shall come next week to ask your mother for her daughter's hand. Will she be willing to give you to me?'

Alicia bit her lip. 'She probably won't be, Francesco. She expects me to go to college.'

'For the love of God, do not ask me to wait that long for you, Alicia.' He kissed her with mounting urgency. 'Life is short, *carissima*,' he said against her lips. 'Let us not waste any of it apart. Fate meant us to be together. Do you not believe this?'

Alicia did believe it, utterly. But trying to make her mother believe it would be another matter. 'Bron will take some persuading,' she warned.

'You call her by her name?' he said, diverted.

'Yes.' Alicia hesitated. 'You'll probably be surprised when you meet her. She looks too young to be my mother.' She took in a deep breath. 'Francesco, if we really are going to be married—'

'You doubt this?' he demanded, and kissed her hard. 'Believe it, *amore*. You will be my wife as soon as it can be arranged.'

'You'd better learn a bit more about me first.'

'Nothing you could tell me would change my mind,' he assured her.

CHAPTER THREE

To HIS credit it had not, Alicia conceded now as she reached the hotel chosen as the venue for the party. She handed her raincoat in, then hurried off to the flower-banked function room overlooking Cardiff Bay. She checked with the catering manager, to be told the waitresses were ready to serve the canapés, and the waiters were lined up at the bar, champagne bottles at the ready. At her signal the pianist began to play, and she returned to the entrance to smile in welcome as the first batch of guests arrived.

'Looking good, Alicia,' said the managing director jovially. 'Excellent job.'

'Thank you.' She smiled, pleased.

For the next hour Alicia's entire attention was focussed on making sure that everything ran to plan, and that the press had access not only to the sponsor's management but to all the celebrities, rugby and otherwise, who were present. Satisfied that drinks were circulating fast enough, she checked that dinner would be served on time—welcome news, since her only meal that day had been a sketchy breakfast. As she rejoined the party the marketing director, who had once played at centre for Cardiff, caught her by the arm.

'Come with me, my fair Alicia,' said David Rees-Jones. 'A guy's just arrived who says he knows you. I played against him once in a game against Italy.'

She stiffened, alarm bells ringing as David relentlessly towed her through the crowd to join the man at one of the great windows looking down on the water. 'You remember Francesco da Luca? How come you two know each other?'

Alicia's eyes narrowed in fierce warning at Francesco.

'We met years ago in Florence,' he said smoothly, and took her hand to kiss it. '*Com'esta*, Alicia? You look very beautiful tonight.'

'She looks beautiful every night, friend,' said David cheerfully, and with a wink at Alicia excused himself to greet some late arrivals.

'What are you doing here?' she hissed, pinning on a bright, social smile.

Francesco's triumphant answering smile set her teeth on edge. 'I was invited.'

'By David?'

'No.' He manoeuvred her nearer the window, neatly isolating her from the rest of the room. 'Last night I dined with some old rugby friends who introduced me to John Griffiths. He was most kind to invite me here tonight.'

Alicia stared, seething, through the window. If his invitation had come from the managing director, she had to grin and bear it. Even if it choked her. 'Are you here long?' she asked politely, as though they were strangers.

'For as long as necessary,' said Francesco with emphasis, and moved closer. 'I insist that we talk tonight, Alicia.'

She turned narrowed, hostile eyes on him. 'Insist?'

He laid a hand on his heart. '*Mi dispiace. Request* is better?'

'No. As far as I'm concerned, we have nothing to talk about.'

'But we do, Alicia.' He took her hand. 'I will take you home when the party is over.'

She shook her head. 'The party was over for us a long time ago, Francesco.'

His grasp tightened. 'Ah no, *contessa*, you are mistaken.'

'Neither mistaken nor interested, Francesco. And don't call me that! Now, let me go, please. Dinner is about to be served.' Not that she felt hungry any more.

'Wait,' he commanded. 'Why did your mother move from Blake Street?'

Conscious of curious eyes turned in their direction, Alicia kept her smile pinned in place as though they were just indulging in party chat. 'She got married.'

His eyes softened as he released her. 'And do you like her husband?'

'Yes, very much. Now, I've got to go—'

'Not until you tell me where you live.'

Oh well. He had to know sometime. 'I rent a flat right here in the Bay.'

'You live alone there?'

She nodded curtly, and hurried off through the crowd.

It seemed like hours before the meal and the speeches were finally over. At last Alicia collected her raincoat and went down to the foyer, where most of the management and their wives and partners were waiting for taxis. And, with them, Francesco da Luca.

'Well done, Alicia. A triumph for Wales and for the party tonight,' said John Griffiths with satisfaction. 'Can we drop you on our way?'

'I have a taxi waiting,' said Francesco swiftly.

'Ah. We leave her in good hands, then.'

Goodnights were exchanged, and before Alicia could argue that she lived near enough to walk home she was giving a taxi driver her address, which Francesco noted down in something he took from his wallet. He needed the information anyway, thought Alicia, resigned. Ever since Bron's surprise marriage and her move to her husband's home in Cowbridge, there had been no way for Francesco to demand news of his missing bride. And presumably he wanted to marry again and provide an heir for Montedaluca. In which case he could just send her the necessary papers to sign and that would be that. Mission accomplished.

The ridiculously short journey was accomplished in fraught silence, which lasted after Francesco paid the driver and contin-ued as he followed Alicia into the lift in the foyer of her waterside building. By the time the doors opened at her floor, every nerve in her body was tied in knots.

When she ushered him into her sitting room, Francesco made straight for the glass doors which opened onto a minuscule balcony overlooking the Bay. He turned to her with a smile. 'You also have a room with a view, Alicia.'

'It's why I couldn't resist the flat,' she admitted, ignoring the memory his words brought to life. 'Though the basement swimming-pool and parking facilities make it worth the steep rent.' She gave him a bright smile. 'Would you like some coffee, or a drink? I can give you some passable wine.'

'*Grazie*, nothing.' He looked round the room, at the small sofa and the one chair that could be remotely described as comfortable. 'Let us sit down.'

Alicia took off her raincoat, and conscious, now that she was alone with Francesco, that her caramel silk shift stopped short of her knees and left one shoulder bare, excused herself to put her raincoat away. Feeling defenceless without it, she snatched up an elderly black cardigan and wrapped herself in it to rejoin her uninvited guest.

She took the chair and waved him to the sofa. 'All right, Francesco. But I warn you, I'm tired. So I hope this won't take long.'

He sat down, eyeing the cardigan in amusement. 'If that garment is meant to hide you from me, Alicia, it does not succeed.' His eyes moved over her in slow, nerve-jangling scrutiny. 'You have changed much from the shy young girl I first met.'

He had changed too. His face was harder, older, but no less striking than the first time she'd seen it, caught on camera in grinning triumph. 'I grew up, Francesco. It took me longer than most girls, but the treatment you and the *contessa* dished out fast-forwarded me into adulthood pretty rapidly in the end.'

Francesco's jaw clenched. 'My mother is dead,' he reminded her.

'And, as I said in my letter, I'm truly sorry for your loss.'

'Are you?'

'Of course. She was the most important person in your life. You must miss her very much.'

'I do. But I do not pretend that, now she is dead, she was a saint.' He sighed heavily. 'I regret that she did not welcome you to our home with warmth.'

That was an understatement for the permafrost which had chilled Alicia to the bone. She shrugged. 'But she was right when she told me I was an unsuitable bride for her son.'

His eyebrows shot up. 'Mamma said this to you?'

'I'm sure she said it to you, too.'

'*Davverro*, but I made it plain to her that you were the only bride *I* wanted.'

She raised a sceptical eyebrow. 'A pity you didn't make it plainer to me. Once I arrived in Montedaluca, I began to doubt it more with every passing day. Most people in the *castello* took their cue from the *contessa* and made me feel like an outsider. Which I was, of course. Apart from your great-aunt Luisa, and the lady you hired to teach me Italian, hardly anyone spoke to me for the six weeks I lived there—including you. You were so busy during the run-up to the wedding you had no time for me. You turned into a stranger.' Alicia smiled coldly. 'Which you were, of course. Until then, I didn't even know you had a title.'

He shrugged dismissively. 'Such things mean little now.'

'It meant a great deal to your mother. The only time she deigned to spend with me was filled with instructions on how a future Contessa da Luca must behave.' Alicia smiled sardonically. 'She must have been utterly delighted when I bolted.'

He shook his head. 'You are wrong. She was ravaged with worry.'

'You surprise me. I thought she would have been over the moon because you were free again.'

'But I am not free.' His mouth twisted. 'Having married you in the *cattedrale* in Montedaluca, I am bound to you for life.'

Alicia's eyes flashed. 'Cut the drama, Francesco. You can get a divorce easily enough. Or easier still you could just get the marriage annulled after what happened—or didn't happen—between us.'

'No one knows this,' he said, his tone so harsh it startled her. 'Unless you told your mother, or Megan?'

Alicia shivered and drew the cardigan closer. 'How could I bear to talk about—about *that* to anyone?'

'So what reason did you give your mother for leaving me?'

'I said I'd made a huge mistake; that it was better to make a clean break right away.' She smiled. 'Bron, not surprisingly, wished I'd decided before the ceremony rather than after, but she sympathised totally with my refusal to return to Montedaluca. The *contessa* was no warmer to her than she was to me, even though Bron did her the courtesy of agreeing to hold the wedding in Montedaluca instead of Cardiff.'

'But Signora Cross soon had her revenge,' he said grimly.

Alicia frowned. 'How, exactly?'

'When my mother accompanied me to Cardiff to see her—'

'She did *what*?'

Francesco's eyes narrowed. 'You did not know this?'

'I most certainly did not!'

'It was very soon after you left me, Alicia.'

She stared at him in blank astonishment.

'You do not believe me?' He shrugged. 'It is the truth. Your mother swore to me that you had gone away.'

Alicia regrouped hurriedly. 'I had. When I got back from Paris I was so—so miserable I was sent off with Megan to stay with her grandmother in Hay-on-Wye for a while to recover. Or try to.'

Francesco's jaw tightened. 'I was told nothing of this during the visit. Megan's parents were there to support your mother. Also the large brother.' He smiled grimly. 'They were unmoved by my anguish. Your mother insisted that you never wanted to see me again.'

Alicia stared at him, shaken, feeling the warmth drain from her face.

'You are very pale. Do you have brandy, Alicia?' asked

Francesco gently. He got up to take her by the hand and led her to the sofa.

'No.' She tried to smile, but her lips were stiff. 'I'll make some tea in a minute.'

'Tell me what to do and I will make it,' he commanded.

'No. First I just need to sit and get my head round this.'

Francesco sat beside her, keeping tight hold of her hand. 'I swear it is the truth, Alicia.'

'I'm sure it is. It would be easy enough to disprove. But it's a shock, just the same,' she said huskily, her throat thickening. 'I just wish I'd known.'

'*Piangi!*' he ordered, and held her close.

Alicia obeyed, but not for long. She blew her nose in the handkerchief Francesco produced, but when she tried to move away he held her tightly, one hand sliding under the ancient cardigan to smooth over the silk covering her shoulders.

'No, *piccola*. Stay. It is easier to talk like this, no?'

Oh, yes. Half seduced by his touch, the mixed pain and pleasure of his endearment made it all too dangerously easy. *But*, a voice in her brain quickly reminded her, although his mother had been partly to blame for her headlong escape from matrimony it had been Francesco's words that had actually sent his bride on the run. Words that had remained, engraved in her mind, ever since. Alicia pushed at his restraining arms until he released her, then went back to the chair. Sniffing inelegantly, she mopped away the last of her tears and smiled at him in bleak apology as she drew the cardigan closer.

'I'm afraid I've ruined your handkerchief.'

'*Gran Dio*, what does that matter?' His eyes glittered like blue flames. 'When you ran from me you ruined my life!'

Alicia met the look head on. 'I thought I was giving it back to you, *Signor Conte*. I was sure you'd go back to your mamma and Montedaluca, glad to be free of your unsatisfactory bride. I'm sure the *contessa* was thrilled.'

'As I have told you,' he said harshly, 'she was not.'

'I find that hard to believe.'

'Nevertheless, it is the truth. When she saw my despair, my mother confessed to much regret that she had not behaved well towards you.'

'To a "freckled schoolgirl with red hair and a figure like a boy",' quoted Alicia with deadly accuracy.

Faint colour rose along Francesco's patrician cheekbones. 'You overheard?'

'Except for the Italian for freckles, which I already knew, your mother took good care to speak English.'

'So that the servants would not understand,' he said stiffly.

'But that *I* would.' Alicia shrugged. 'Not that it matters any more, Francesco. That schoolgirl grew up fast.'

'And no longer has a figure like a boy.'

'Nor was my hair ever red!' That was something which had annoyed her almost as much as the rest of the *contessa*'s comments had hurt.

His eyes moved over her with a look as tactile as a caress. 'You have matured into an alluring woman, and I was not the only man who thought so tonight.'

'I see a lot of men in my work,' she said indifferently.

The eyes slitted. 'Is there one you see more than others?'

'Several I look on as friends to share a meal with.'

'And a bed?' he demanded.

'You have no right to ask me that!'

'I have every right,' he said through his teeth. 'I am your husband.'

'You gave up any right to call yourself that on our wedding night,' she shot back.

He took in a deep, unsteady breath. 'Alicia, in my frustration and *disilluzione*, I uttered words I have regretted bitterly through all the years since. If you could have witnessed my anguish when I found you gone, you would have had your revenge.'

She shrugged impatiently. 'I wanted escape, not revenge.'

'And threw your rings on the floor!'

'Better than having theft added to my sins,' she retorted. 'I scrubbed myself, pulled on my old clothes and ran off via the service lift with my back pack, desperate to get away before you came back.'

'You had no thought that I would be demented, thinking of you alone in Paris?' Francesco's jaw tightened. 'I was such an ogre, Alicia?'

She shrugged. 'If not an ogre, you were nothing like the man I fell in love with. Though the change had started long before then. When I arrived to stay in Montedaluca before the wedding, you were different, so preoccupied with your business affairs, that you had very little time for me. Almost from the start I began to wonder if I was making a big mistake. But I just didn't have the courage to put a stop to all the preparations your mother had made. Afterwards I wished to God I had. You said such terrible things; I was heartbroken. But not for long,' she added quickly. 'My heart soon healed once I cut you out of it.'

They stared at each other in tense silence.

'So. Tell me what happened next,' said Francesco at last.

'Not much. I spent a long time with Meg, pulling myself together, then I had another holiday alone with Bron in Cornwall. And then I went to college. Only not here in Cardiff, as originally planned.'

'Because you thought I might trace you there?'

She gave a flippant little laugh. 'Heavens no, that never occurred to me. I knew you'd rung Bron a few times to ask about me, but because you never came after me—or so I thought—I assumed you were glad to get shot of me. I transferred to the university where Megan was reading law, and I changed to economics because by then an art-history degree with a year's study in Florence was the last thing I wanted.' She smiled at him sardonically. 'You wouldn't have recognised the convent schoolgirl, Francesco. I was the archetypal student—with body piercing, bare midriff even in the dead of winter, and skirts so short they terrified my mother. I dyed multi-coloured streaks in my hair, drank beer in the union with the rugby team, and partied like mad.'

He sat very still, his eyes locked with hers. 'You held me responsible for this?'

Alicia nodded vehemently. 'Of course I did. But after a while Bron read the riot act, and told me I was worrying Megan so much her work was suffering, which meant her parents were worried too. So I put you out of my mind, cut the partying and got down to work myself.'

'And in time my pride would no longer allow me to continue pleading with Signora Cross for news of you,' Francesco said bitterly. 'She is a very strong lady.'

'Life has shaped her that way.'

'She has never told you more about your father?'

'No.' Suddenly Alicia could take no more. 'Enough of this, Francesco. Would you please go now?'

He got up at once. '*Va bene.* But I will take you to lunch tomorrow.'

She shook her head. 'Sorry. I'm having lunch with Megan.'

'Then I shall come here in the evening.' His eyes locked on hers. 'Make very sure you are here, Alicia. I will not return to Montedaluca until the problem is resolved.'

'Oh, very well,' she said wearily. 'But come after dinner, please.' No way was she going to prepare a meal for him. 'Do you want to ring for a taxi?'

'No.' His jaw tightened. 'I will relieve you of my unwanted company immediately. *A domani.*'

'Goodnight.' Well aware that she'd offended him, Alicia saw him to the door. She locked up and turned out the lights, and with a grateful sigh made for her bedroom, suddenly so tired it was a struggle to go through her usual routine before she crawled into bed.

An hour later she gave up all idea of sleeping and got up again, cursing Francesco for spoiling what should have been a wonderful day. Wales had beaten Italy—which for her was a particularly personal triumph—and the party she'd organised had been a success, except for the presence of Francesco da Luca. She should have been on cloud nine. Alicia sighed irritably, made some tea, propped up the pillows on her bed and sat upright against them, unable to get the da Lucas' visit to her mother out of her mind. In the morning she would ring Bron to get her side of the story before Francesco returned tomorrow night. Bronwen Cross had obviously not wanted her daughter to go back to her bridegroom.

But Alicia felt no animosity towards her mother, who early on in life had learned to make her own way. Bronwen Cross's father had died when she was twelve, and her mother a relatively short time later during Bron's first year at Cardiff University. At the time the newly-orphaned Bronwen was lodging in the home of Huw and Eira Davies in a room in the attic flat they let out to students to help pay the mortgage on their Victorian town house.

Huw Davies was a solicitor, and in spite of the long hours he worked in his aim to achieve partnership in his firm he was a godsend to his grieving young lodger in sorting out the legalities after the death of her mother. In exchange Bron looked after his young son, Gareth, during Eira's trips to the ante-natal clinic at nearby Glossop Terrace, the hospital where the second Davies baby would soon be born.

After Megan had arrived Bron was only too happy to continue with her babysitting services, and soon became so much a part of the family that, when she discovered to her horror that she herself was pregnant, it was to Eira that she turned in despair. There was no question of abortion for someone of Bron's faith, nor of giving her baby up for adoption. She also flatly refused to name the father, or to ask him for support as Huw urged, but due to a modest inheritance from her mother Bron was able to rent the entire attic flat of the house in Blake Street and carry on at university. And when Alicia was born at the end of September, in good time for the autumn term, Eira volunteered to look after her along with her own children for a small fee the young mother insisted on. It was an arrangement which not only suited everyone, but allowed Bron to combine motherhood with studying for a fine-arts degree.

Alicia sighed. From earliest memory she'd had two mothers, since Eira Davies had always treated her as one of her own. To add to the mix, Alicia had a ready-made brother and sister from the start in Gareth and Megan, and, because the toddlers referred to their much-loved babysitter as 'Bron', as soon as she could talk Alicia did the same.

Her background, or lack of it, had been a huge part of Alicia's ineligibility from Contessa Sophia da Luca's point of view. As if freckles, dimples, 'red' hair and lack of curves were not enough, her son's *fidanzata* was the child of a single mother and unknown father. Bad news all round from the *contessa*'s point of view. Though, to be fair to Francesco, he had not cared about Alicia's lack of pedigree. His sole objection had been to a bride who was so far from his expectations on their wedding night his outraged reaction had ended their marriage before it began. And since that fateful evening in Paris Alicia had never laid eyes on Francesco again until today at the Millennium Stadium in Cardiff.

CHAPTER FOUR

ALICIA slept so late next morning there was no answer when she rang her mother. Frustrated, she left a message for Bron and went off to lunch in Blake Street.

'Rhys has just nipped out with Gareth,' Meg said, hugging Alicia. 'So, how did the party go?'

'Like clockwork, thank heavens.' Alicia hesitated, but left any mention of Francesco until they were all together. 'Mum and Dad still in Hay?'

Meg nodded soberly. 'Grandma's not too good, so the parents are staying put there for the time being.'

Which right now left Gareth as the only available eye-witness to the *contessa*'s visit. Alicia would have preferred to speak to her mother first, but she needed answers before tonight's encounter with Francesco. She kept up a flow of chatter to describe the party as she helped a rather subdued Meg with the lunch, and when the two men came back the four of them sat down to eat in the dining room, in the bay window looking out on the garden.

'Posh today,' commented Gareth as Rhys, the trainee surgeon, carved the roast.

'It's not often the four of us are together any more,' said Meg, passing vegetables. 'Besides, yesterday's triumph calls for something more special than the kitchen table.'

'Amen to that,' agreed her brother, eyeing Alicia as he filled her glass. 'You look tired today, *cariad*.'

'Big day yesterday.'

'Was your party a success?' asked Rhys.

Alicia nodded. 'It certainly was. Not a hitch. Though for the money the company shelled out that's hardly surprising.'

'Talking of money, people, we've found a house,' said Rhys, then rolled his eyes as his wife glared at him. 'Wasn't I supposed to say that?'

'I wanted to break the news myself,' Megan said crossly, but smiled at him to soften the blow. 'The house is in Heath, Lally. My hot-shot surgeon will be able to tumble straight out of bed into his shift at the hospital.'

'Why the hell do you want to saddle yourself with a mortgage at this stage in your career?' demanded Gareth.

'Because I have this clever, trainee-solicitor wife who is willing to support me until I actually *am* a hot-shot surgeon. And, although we have great digs here with your parents, we want a home of our own,' said Rhys, and leaned over to kiss Megan.

'For goodness' sake,' said Gareth in disgust. 'Shouldn't you two be over the lovebird stage by now?'

'Killjoy!' jeered Alicia, and smiled encouragement at the other two. 'Don't mind the crusty old bachelor here; it's sweet to see a married couple billing and cooing.'

Gareth raised a sardonic eyebrow. 'You, of course, being such an expert on marriage.'

'Pig!' snapped Megan, glaring at him. 'Take no notice, Lally. He's in a snit because his latest squeeze has just dumped him.'

'Oh, bad luck.' Alicia smiled at Gareth sweetly. 'Did I ever hear this one's name?'

'Dawn, wasn't it?' asked Rhys.

Megan shook her head. 'That was the last one.'

'Her name is Julie,' said Gareth shortly. 'And we parted by mutual consent.'

'Which means she wanted an engagement ring,' said his cynical sister. 'Who's for pudding?'

After the meal Alicia sent the men into the sitting room to

watch a recording of the previous day's victory while she helped Megan clear up.

'That was gorgeous, Meg. Your mother couldn't have done better.'

'Praise indeed!' Megan eyed her anxiously as she switched on the dishwasher. 'Something's wrong, isn't it?'

'You could say that.' Alicia braced herself. 'I bumped into Francesco at the stadium yesterday.'

Meg sat down at the kitchen table with a thump. 'What happened?'

'I cut him dead at first, but he nobbled me after the match, insisting we talk.'

'What did he say?'

'Not a lot, really. We had a brief argument outside the stadium, then he let me go on my way, or so I thought. But he turned up at the party last night and insisted on taking me home.'

'So he knows where you live now?' Meg shot her a troubled glance. 'What did he want? Or shouldn't I ask?'

'If you mean was he after my body, no. But he's coming back to the flat to see me tonight. To settle things.'

'About a divorce?'

Alicia nodded. 'Though why he's taken all this time to get round to it beats me. Maybe because he's a Catholic.'

Meg rolled her eyes. 'And how! The full nuptial-mass at your wedding was overpowering. Or was it all those lilies in the church?'

'Probably the waves of disapproval wafting over to us from the *contessa*.' Alicia pulled her up. 'Come on, let's join the men. I need to grill Gareth about something.'

Rhys paused the tape as they went into Eira Davies's comfortable sitting room. 'I don't suppose you angels made coffee?' he said hopefully.

'You're right, we didn't,' his wife agreed. 'Sit down. Alicia has something to say.'

Gareth patted the sofa beside him. 'Then she can come and sit by me to say it.'

Alicia shook her head and perched on the arm of the chair opposite him so she could look him in the eye. 'Yesterday I was late joining you at the match because I bumped into Francesco da Luca on my way into the stadium.'

Gareth started up, but she waved him back.

'Sit down and listen, please.'

'So what did the Count of Monte Cristo have to say for himself?' sneered Gareth.

'Not much at the time. But he turned up at the party last night, and insisted on taking me home.'

'What was he after? A spot of auld lang syne between the sheets?' Three pairs of eyes regarded Gareth with such distaste that he shrugged a defiant apology. 'Sorry. Go on, Lally, what happened?'

'Francesco informed me,' said Alicia evenly, 'that very soon after I ran away from him he brought his mother here to Blake Street to look for me.'

'*What?* Is that true?' Meg gaped at her in astonishment. 'When was this?'

'While I was in Hay with you.' Alicia looked pointedly at Gareth. 'You would know exactly when, I believe.'

Meg rounded on her brother in fury. 'You were actually here when they came? And never said anything?'

Gareth flung up his hands. 'Hey, back off. It wasn't my fault. Bron swore us to silence about his visit. She said Alicia had finished with da Luca for good, and made us promise not to let him know where she was.' He eyed Alicia uncomfortably. 'I wasn't happy about it. I don't like the man, but he looked so bloody desperate that day I couldn't help feeling sorry for him. And even the *contessa* looked as though she'd had all the stuffing knocked out of her.'

Alicia slid from the arm of the chair to the seat, feeling much the same way.

'I can't believe you never said a word, Gareth Davies,' said Meg hotly. 'You knew how unhappy Lally was at the time.'

'Of course I did. But I thought Francesco was the one who'd

made her unhappy!' He shot a look at Alicia. 'Now the subject's finally come up, he didn't—well—hurt you, did he, *cariad*?'

'Knock me about, you mean?'

'Hell, no, I never thought that. I meant—'

She put up a hand. 'I assure you that Francesco never laid a finger on me.'

'So why the devil did you run away?' demanded Gareth.

'That's nothing to do with you,' protested Megan.

'It is if she thinks I'm somehow to blame!' he retorted.

'Of course you're not to blame,' said Alicia impatiently. 'I just had to know if Francesco was telling me the truth last night. And Bron wasn't in when I rang her this morning, so you were the only one available that I could ask.'

'Mum and Dad knew about this *all along*?' demanded Meg, and rounded on her husband. 'Did you know, Rhys?'

'Of course I didn't,' he said indignantly. '*I* wouldn't have kept it from you.'

'I had no choice,' snapped Gareth. 'Dad is Bron's solicitor, remember, so he not only had to keep quiet himself, he made Mum and me swear to keep the secret too.' He gave Alicia an uneasy look. 'I honestly thought it was for the best.'

'Because you didn't want Alicia to marry Francesco in the first place. Or anyone else, for that matter,' said Megan tartly.

Gareth glared at his sister, then turned to Alicia as he got to his full, considerable height. 'Look, I did what Bron asked because I thought it was what *you* wanted. End of story. Thanks for lunch, Megan. So long, all; I'm off.'

When Alicia got back to her flat a message was waiting from her mother, asking her to ring back.

'Sorry I missed you earlier, darling. George took me out for a meal. You had lunch with Megan as planned?'

Alicia rang to give her mother a brief description of the party, confirmed that her dress had been a success, then braced herself. 'Mother, I met someone at the match yesterday.'

Silence for a moment. 'If I'm *Mother*, for once, this is obviously not good news.'

'It was Francesco. He was there to support his home team.'

Bron inhaled deeply. 'I suppose it was bound to happen some day. What did he want?'

'I'm not sure. But he certainly surprised me with one bit of information. Apparently he took his mother to Blake Street to look for me soon after I left him.'

More silence. 'Yes, darling, he did,' said Bron at last, clearing her throat. 'And now you've found out you're furious because I kept quiet about it.'

'Absolutely right. Honestly, Mother,' said Alicia hotly. 'Did it never occur to you that it would have helped me enormously to know that both Francesco and the *contessa* had cared enough to fly to Cardiff to look for me?'

'No, not for a minute. You said you wanted nothing more to do with him,' Bron reminded her.

'Even so, you had no right to keep his visit a secret.'

'I did what *I* thought was right. To protect you. You flatly refused to say why you ran away so I took it for granted Francesco had, well, abused you in some way.'

'No, Mother, he most certainly had not.' Or, if he had, only with words.

'Tell me, darling,' said Bron after a pause. 'What exactly would you have done if you'd known Francesco came to look for you?'

Alicia thought it over. 'Probably nothing. It was the fact that his mother came too that made the difference.'

'Why?'

'Because it meant that she felt some regret about the way she'd treated me.'

'It gave me tremendous personal satisfaction to refuse her,' said Bron, with such relish that Alicia's eyes widened.

'So it wasn't just to protect me, then—it was also to get back at her.'

'I'm only human.'

'So am I! Which is why it would have meant so much to me to know about the visit.'

'It's the only secret I kept, darling. I've reported every one of Francesco's calls since. And, in case you're wondering, there haven't been any for quite a while.'

'I know. Apparently his pride kicked in at some point and said "enough".'

'I'm surprised that for a man like Francesco that didn't happen sooner. Look, darling, if I did the wrong thing I'm sorry. Come to lunch next Sunday. Or, better still, come before then so I can grovel in person.'

'No grovelling required. As you said, you did what you thought was the right thing. I'll see you on Sunday.'

Alicia switched off the phone and sat by the balcony doors to look out over her bit of Cardiff Bay. A picture of the *contessa*, faultlessly dressed and ramrod straight in the seldom-used drawing room at Blake Street, was suddenly vivid. How tense it must have been, with the Davies trio supporting Bron against Francesco and his mother. And how immensely difficult the *contessa* must have found it to beg for news of the runaway bride. While Bron, by the sound of it, had taken infinite pleasure in sending Francesco and the *contessa* packing with no news at all.

Alicia got up at last, feeling more like taking a nap than getting ready for the encounter with Francesco. She took a long shower instead, and afterwards pulled her hair up in a cruelly tight knot and put on black jeans, a sweater, and high-heeled boots, her lipstick the only touch of colour. At last she set a tray with glasses and a bottle of wine in a cooler bucket, and sat by the window with a book to wait until the doorbell rang.

'Francesco,' said a voice over the intercom just before eight. Alicia buzzed him in, then stood in her open doorway to wait for him. Francesco was also in sweater and jeans, which, like his leather jacket and gleaming hand-made shoes, were black like hers. And he looked so darkly handsome a hot streak of startling—and utterly mortifying—response shot through her at the sight of him.

'*Buona sera,*' he said quietly.

Alicia irritably reined in the libido she was normally unaware she even possessed. 'Hi. Come in. Would you like wine, or coffee?'

'*Grazie*; a glass of wine would be most welcome.' He took the opener she handed him and dealt efficiently with the bottle.

'Thank you.' Alicia gave a glass of wine to Francesco, then made for the chair with her own. 'Do sit down.'

He sat on the sofa, and raised his glass in toast. '*Salute.*'

Alicia drank a little, then set her glass down. 'I spoke to my mother today. She confirmed that you took the *contessa* to Blake Street.'

He smiled sardonically. 'Ah. So now you believe me?'

'Oh, I believed you right away, Francesco. I merely rang Bron to ask why she never told me about it.'

His eyes narrowed. 'I am most interested to hear what she said.'

Alicia looked at him squarely. 'She thought I bolted because you'd abused me in some way.'

His eyes blazed with instant outrage. '*Cosa?* She thought I hurt you?'

'You did hurt me, Francesco.'

'*Daverro*, but I did not touch you! *Gran Dio!*' He slammed the wine glass down on the table beside him, smouldering at her. 'She believed I forced myself on you?'

She shook her head impatiently. 'If she did I certainly never told her that. I didn't know until today that anyone had even considered the possibility.'

'Anyone?' He pounced. 'Who else thought this?'

'Gareth Davies. He was at Megan's today. Like Bron, he believed it was something you did that sent me running for home. Which is true, but it was nothing physical.'

He picked up the glass and drained it, his lids half-veiling his eyes. 'And did you make this clear to your mother—*and* to Megan's brother?'

'Of course I did.'

'*Eccelente.*' He was silent for a moment, then shrugged. 'So.

Since I am now cleared of one crime, at least, it is time for the serious talk, Alicia.'

'Talk away. You want a divorce, I assume.'

Francesco shot her a veiled, unsettling look. 'Do you?'

'Of course.'

'So that you can marry again?'

She shook her head. 'As I told you before, marriage holds no appeal for me.'

'You are content to live your life alone?'

Alicia finished her wine and raised limpid eyes to his. 'What makes you think I do that?'

Francesco's smile set her teeth on edge. 'No man shares such a small flat, Alicia.'

'True. But the bedroom is quite big enough for two. When the occasion arises,' she added deliberately.

He stared at her in taut silence, then got up to refill their glasses. 'I have never seen you in black before. You look very stern, very cold tonight, Alicia.'

'These are my working clothes.'

Francesco's mouth twisted. 'You mean you did not dress to please me.'

'I always dress to please myself!'

'The dress you wore last night pleased every man who saw it.'

Alicia shrugged impatiently. 'Look, Francesco, just get on with it and tell me what you want.'

'*Va bene.*' He leaned back on the sofa. 'I came to Cardiff this weekend to support the rugby, it is true, but I also made the vow that this time I would not leave until I found out where you live. So before I left Montedaluca I rang your mother in Blake Street.'

'You had no luck, then.'

'Ah, but I did. Megan answered the telephone.'

Alicia stared at him narrowly. 'You spoke to *Meg*?'

'Yes, but I asked her to keep silent. And before you ask,' he said, holding up a hand, 'she did not give me your address, or your telephone number. I told her it was vital that I see you, and after much persuading she told me you would be at the Millennium Stadium for the match. Nothing more, so do not be angry with her.'

'Oh, I'm not angry with *her*,' said Alicia bitterly.

'Only with me! So. Now you know how I found you.'

'But I still don't know why you want to see me. I haven't been hiding, Francesco. Once you were here in Cardiff you could have found my address just by looking in the telephone directory.'

He shrugged. 'This did not occur to me.'

Alicia eyed him challengingly. 'So what exactly do you want?'

His eyes locked with hers. 'I want you—I *need* you—to come back to Montedaluca.'

'What?' She stared back in utter horror. 'No way!'

'It is legally required that you do,' he assured her.

'You mean I actually have to go back there to sign something before you can get a divorce?'

'It is vitally necessary for you to return, yes.' He looked at her intently. 'For years I have carried in my mind the look in your eyes that night.'

'Our wedding night,' she said bitterly.

'Davverro. So before I asked for a divorce I desired very much to know how you were, what you had done with your life. As I have tried so many, many times to discover from Signora Cross,' he added, equally bitter.

Alicia eyed him ruefully. 'You never did call my mother Bron.'

'She did not give me permission to do so.'

'Which is odd, because when she first met you she liked you very much.'

'This is true?' said Francesco, surprised. 'I thought she did not wish you to marry me.'

'Only because you were in such a hurry. Other than taking me to live in another country, you were the ideal husband in her eyes, because you could provide something she'd always wanted for me.'

'Love?'

She shook her head. 'The security she'd lacked herself. But it all went horribly wrong. And because I refused to say why I ran from you she drew the wrong conclusions.'

'After such conclusions,' he said darkly, 'I am amazed she allowed me into the house.'

'She had no choice. You took your mother along.'

His mouth tightened. 'Even so, Megan's brother would have liked to use his fists on me.'

'He told me today that he was a bit sorry for you because you looked so desperate.'

Francesco gave a mirthless laugh. '*E possibile.* But he also wanted to hit me.'

They sat in tense silence for a moment, then Alicia sighed. 'So, now you have met up with me again, and can see that I have a perfectly good life, you can go back to Montedaluca and get on with yours. So start your divorce proceedings, Francesco. As far as I'm concerned, you're a free man.'

'*Mille grazie,*' he said with sarcasm. 'However, it is necessary for you to interrupt this perfect life of yours for a little time to return to Montedaluca. In her will, my mother left you a token of her repentance, and you must take possession of this in person, Alicia, to satisfy the terms of the will.'

She shook her head vehemently. 'Whatever it is, I don't want it. The last gift she gave me was a poisoned chalice. No way do I want another.'

'*Cosa?* I don't understand. What is this poisoned chalice?' demanded Francesco, mystified.

'I was speaking metaphorically.'

'Tell me what you mean!'

'Before we left on our honeymoon the *contessa* sent me a prettily packaged gift, via Cinzia, her maid, with instructions on how to use the contents. I was so pleased.' Alicia's mouth twisted. 'What a naïve little fool I was!'

'Tell me about this present,' he commanded.

'No, Francesco, there's no point. Your mother is no longer

alive, and the past is over and done with.' She got up and went to the window. 'And I flatly refuse to go back to Montedaluca.'

He moved so close behind her she could see the chiselled planes of his face reflected in the window. 'There is a problem. Until you receive this legacy, my mother's will is frozen.'

She spun round with a taunting smile. 'Oh, I *see*. You need the money.'

Francesco said something violent that her Italian lessons had never covered. 'No,' he said through his teeth. 'I, personally, do not. But the other legatees can receive nothing until you take what is yours.'

Alicia's eyes narrowed suspiciously. 'I don't believe you!'

He lifted a shoulder in the gesture she remembered so well. 'As you wish.'

'Is Cinzia one of these legatees?'

'Of course not,' he said, surprised. 'My mother dismissed her the day after the wedding. Why do you ask?'

'Just curiosity. So who, exactly, am I keeping from their bequests?'

'My great-aunt, for one.'

'Zia Luisa is still alive?' Alicia's eyes warmed. 'She was one of the few people at the *castello* who was kind to me. Where is she now?'

'At home in the *castello*—where else?'

Alicia suddenly felt very tired. 'Is all this *really* true, Francesco?'

'That you must come back to Montedaluca? Yes, Alicia.' His eyes softened. 'Is it so terrible a thing to do?'

'The place has unhappy memories for me,' she reminded him. 'And my welcome will be even colder than last time. I left you the day after the wedding, remember.'

His mouth twisted. 'You think I have forgotten this?'

'No. And that's exactly what I mean. No one else will have forgotten, either. They must all hate me.'

'No one hates you, Alicia. Besides, it is different now. I pensioned off the oldest servants after my mother died. A man on his own has no need of a large staff.'

'Surely you still have Giacomo?'

'Of course,' Francesco agreed dryly. 'He thinks I cannot survive alone. And he is probably right. He has run the *castello* for so long, I cannot imagine life there without him. Bianca Giusti also lives there permanently now she is a widow. She is companion to Zia Luisa. Pina still rules the kitchen, and Antonio the gardens. There is also a young girl, Teresa, who helps Pina or Giacomo as required. They all wait for their bequests,' he added significantly.

Alicia looked at him in silence for so long that Francesco became restive.

'So. You will come?' he demanded.

She sighed. 'It seems I have no choice. But there are conditions,' she added quickly. 'First, I can't get away until after the home rugby games.'

'*Va bene,*' he agreed quickly, a swiftly veiled flash of triumph in his eyes.

'Also, warn your lawyer that whatever legal papers are necessary must be ready and waiting for me to sign as soon as I arrive.' Her chin lifted. 'I refuse to stay longer than a day or two, Francesco. Also, if it's legally necessary to release the other bequests, I will accept whatever the *contessa* has left me. But I won't keep it.'

'You must do with it as you wish,' he said coldly, and got up. '*Allora*, tell me what date is convenient for you to travel and I shall arrange a flight for you.'

'No need. I'll do that myself.'

'Since you have so graciously consented to come,' he said with irony, 'I will not put you to the expense of a plane ticket.' He arched an eyebrow. 'I assume it must be in the name of Miss Alicia Cross, not La Contessa da Luca?'

'You assume right! That was your mother's title.'

'It is also yours.' He bent and took her hand to pull her to her feet. 'Whether it pleases you or not, you are still married to me, Alicia.'

'It takes more than a few lines on paper and a church full of lilies to make a woman feel married,' she retorted.

Francesco's eyes flared dangerously. 'I know other ways to achieve this.' He pulled her close. 'Shall I demonstrate, *sposa mia*?'

'Certainly not,' she snapped, and wrenched away before he could feel her response to his lean, graceful body.

'Che peccato!' He turned away to shrug into his jacket. 'I will also not put you to the expense of a phone call to Montedaluca; therefore, I will contact you to learn when it is convenient for you to travel. What time is best for me to ring?'

'Early evening. If I'm not here, leave a message.'

She scribbled her numbers on the pad by the phone and tore off the sheet to give to him.

'Grazie.' He smiled in warning. 'But remember, Alicia—if I cannot find you I shall apply to Megan again.'

'Leave Megan out of this!'

'Do not be angry with your charming friend. The blame is all mine.' Francesco took her by the shoulders, looked at her mouth long enough to set her pulse racing, then kissed her swiftly on each cheek. *'Arrivederci.'*

She stood very still for a while after the door closed while she willed her pulse back to normal, and then took a deep breath and walked across the room to pick up the phone.

'Hello, Lally,' said Megan fearfully.

'I hope you hadn't gone to bed.'

'Not much point. I knew you'd ring tonight. Francesco told you, then?'

'Yes.'

'Are you horribly angry with me?'

Alicia sighed. 'No. But I just wish you'd said something today.'

'I couldn't. I'd not only promised Francesco, at that point I hadn't told Rhys.'

'Hadn't told me what?' said a voice in the background.

'That I'd talked to Francesco, darling.'

Rhys took over the phone. 'Don't be angry with her, Lally. When Francesco said there was a will to sort out, my legal eagle here thought he should be given the chance to speak to you. She didn't dare say a word in front of Gareth.'

'Because he would have shouted at her, and you wouldn't have stood for that, and there would have been blood on the carpet. He stormed off in a strop as it was,' said Alicia, chuckling. 'Put her back on.'

'So what happened?' asked Megan, sounding a little happier.

Alicia told her in detail.

'No! Are you really going to Montedaluca again?'

'Not happily. But a bunch of elderly legatees can't get their bit until I claim mine, apparently, so I don't have much choice.'

'Francesco didn't say you'd have to go back there. Damn, I wish I'd kept my big mouth shut now,' said Megan with remorse. 'When will you go?'

'After the home rugby games finish. I was taking a couple of weeks off then, anyway. Francesco's paying my air fare. And to rattle my cage he even suggested booking it as La Contessa da Luca!'

'Well, legally you're still married to him.'

'Not for long, Mrs Evans. I shall sign whatever dotted line is necessary to get myself unmarried the moment I get there and that will be that. He'll be out of my life for good.' Alicia gave an unsteady little laugh. 'If only we'd gone to Spain or France for our reward holiday, Meg. Life would have been so much less complicated.'

'True.' Meg heaved a sigh. 'I'm so glad you're not mad at me, Lally.'

'As if! Anyway, Francesco was very much against that. He's a big fan of yours.'

'I like him, too. I just wish—'

'None of that. It's late, and time you were in bed.'

'With me,' said a voice in the background, and Alicia chuckled and wished them both goodnight.

But, when she went to bed herself later, for the first time since she'd moved into the flat the bed seemed empty with no one to share it. Even though, contrary to the impression she'd given Francesco, no one ever had.

CHAPTER FIVE

ALICIA got home next day to find a message from Francesco on her phone.

'I am back in Montedaluca, Alicia. I will ring you tomorrow.'

Which sounded more like a threat than a promise. She pulled the pins from her hair, frowning as the curls sprang free. The prospect of regular phone calls from Francesco as part of life was worrying. Even more worrying, when she'd put him out of that life so completely for so long, was the fact that he was now back there, centre stage. So much so that she'd turned down the offer of dinner tonight with an ex-Saracens rugby player she'd been seeing occasionally when his business trips brought him to Cardiff. Jason had been hinting lately about a closer relationship, but that would mean revealing that she wasn't quite as unattached as he thought. And, since her attachment was not only a husband but also an ex-rugby player, Jason would probably have heard of him.

As though reinforcing his place centre stage, Francesco rang her regularly in the passing days to make sure she was making the necessary arrangements to get away, which made sure she thought of little else.

'I've said I'll come, so I will,' she said crossly one night, cross because he hadn't rung for a couple of nights and she'd stayed at home in case he did.

'I am just making sure. Past experience with you, Alicia, has taught me this,' he informed her.

'Look, Francesco, I've given you the date, so now all you have to do is send the ticket. Or, better still, I'll buy it myself and you can pay me for it later.'

'Ah, no! I cannot trust you to do that. Besides, I have already arranged your flight.'

'Have you, really? When do I fly?'

'Tuesday of next week. And I have a message for you: Zia Luisa is looking forward very much to seeing you again.'

'How sweet of her,' said Alicia, touched. Along with her old Italian teacher, Bianca Giusti, that meant there would at least be two friendly faces at the *castello*.

'So be ready to leave on that day,' he commanded.

'*Si, signore.* Whatever you say!'

'If only that were true, Alicia. *Arrivederci.*'

Instead of waiting in for Francesco to ring, Alicia arranged something for every evening before she left, including a girl's night in with Megan when Rhys was working. But Alicia reserved the final Saturday for a shopping trip with her mother, followed by lunch.

'I enjoyed our morning,' Bron said as they studied a menu afterwards. 'Tiring but productive.'

'I really don't need all this new stuff. I'm not going to be there long,' said Alicia for the umpteenth time.

'It still seems strange to me that you have to go back at all,' said her mother, also not for the first time.

'The peculiarities of Italian law, I suppose. Francesco knew exactly what buttons to push when he told me Zia Luisa and the others wouldn't get their legacy until I take possession of mine. Whatever it may be.'

Bron leaned back in her chair once they'd given their order, elegant as always in a white jacket over a black linen dress, her dark hair in the short, swinging cut she favoured. 'Francesco didn't tell you exactly what the *contessa* had left you?'

'No. Not that it matters. Whatever it is, I shan't keep it.'

Bron frowned. 'I know she wasn't exactly warm towards you, but what did she do to make you so implacable ever since?'

Alicia's face shuttered. 'Let's not spoil our day by talking about it.'

'All right, darling.' Bron grimaced. 'After our recent *froideur* I was afraid you might say no when I suggested some retail therapy.'

Alicia smiled into the vividly attractive face of the woman who looked more like a sister than her mother. 'No way. Without you to rein me in, lord knows what sartorial sins I might commit.'

'True. When it comes to clothes, at least, I know my stuff.'

'No doubt about that. Though you should have seen the *contessa*'s face when I said my mother was making my wedding dress!'

Bron sniffed. 'She expected some botched home-made affair totally unworthy of the Conte da Luca's bride!'

'Absolutely. She did her best to bully me into wearing a creation from the designer she patronised, but since I'd already given in about having the wedding in Montedaluca I put my foot down when it came to the dress. I told her your bridal-wear business was very successful, and no matter what she said I wanted my mother to make my wedding gown. But she had grave doubts right up to the moment she saw me walk down the aisle. The look of relief on her face was priceless.' Alicia frowned. 'I wonder what happened to the dress? I left it at the *castello* when we went away.'

'Do you want it back?'

'Yes, but only because you made it. So if that's the legacy I will accept it.'

When Alicia got back to the flat later there was a message on her phone from the colleague she'd asked round for supper. Maggie had a cold, and thought it wise to keep her unfriendly bacteria to herself.

Alicia rang back to commiserate, then curled up on the sofa with a cup of coffee and a new paperback, perfectly happy at the thought of her first peaceful evening that week. But she didn't say so when Francesco rang.

'How are you, and what have you done today, Alicia?'

'I'm a bit tired. I went on a shopping spree with Bron. We had lunch together, and now she's gone home to George.'

'I trust your mother is well?' he said punctiliously.

'Positively blooming. Matrimony suits her.'

'Unlike her daughter!'

'True. You put me off it for life.'

He drew in a sharp, audible breath. 'You are cruel, Alicia.'

'Hardly surprising, Francesco—I was taught by masters!'

This statement silenced him for so long she began to wonder if they'd been cut off. 'So, what are you doing this evening?' he asked at last.

'I invited a friend round for supper.'

'You are cooking this supper?'

'No. I raided a delicatessen rather than waste time at the stove.' A statement deliberately designed to give Francesco the wrong impression.

'Then I will leave you to enjoy your evening,' he snapped. '*Ciao*, Alicia.'

'*Ciao*, Francesco.'

She smiled to herself as she put the phone down, hoping Francesco would spend his evening wondering about her supper guest while she relaxed alone with a book and a snack, and maybe a film on television later.

Alicia had just finished the supper part of the programme when the doorbell rang. Her eyebrows rose. Most people she knew would be out on the town at this time of night.

To her amazement, her caller was Gareth. 'Come up.' She pressed the release button, then stood in her open doorway, smiling as the familiar figure came bounding up the stairs instead of taking the lift. 'Hey, this is a surprise! I didn't know you were back in town this weekend.'

'No one else does, either,' he said, and took her in his arms and kissed her square on the mouth.

Alicia pulled away, trying to hide her dismayed, knee-jerk rejection. 'So, why am I honoured in particular? Weren't you playing today?' She waved him over to the sofa and sat down in the chair. 'Have you eaten?'

'Yes, thanks. And I did have a match today, but I drove down straight afterwards.' Gareth leaned back against the sofa cushions, eyeing her in unnerving silence.

She swallowed, feeling oddly shaken. Probably because they were so rarely alone together. Like his father and Megan, Gareth's hair and eyes were very dark, but at this particular moment there was something in those Davies eyes that set off alarm bells in Alicia's head. 'So what are you doing back in Cardiff this weekend?' she asked at last, desperate to break the silence.

'After Megan's phone call, I just had to see you.' He leaned forward, accusation in every line of his massive, muscular body. 'Is it true?'

'Is what true?'

'She said you're going back to Montedaluca.'

'That's right.'

His eyes blazed. 'Why? Don't tell me Francesco's persuaded you to go back to him?'

She shook her head impatiently. 'Of course he hasn't. I'm just going back for a day or two to get something the *contessa* left me. Apparently I'm required to take possession of it in person to satisfy the terms of the will.'

He snorted. 'And you actually believe such rot? It's just an excuse for Francesco to get you back in his clutches. Once you're there in his blasted castle again, goodness knows what might happen.' He leaned nearer, his eyes urgent. 'Don't go, *cariad*.'

She shrugged impatiently. 'For heaven's sake, Gareth, I'll only be there a couple of days—just long enough to sort this legacy thing.'

'Then I'll go with you.'

'You most certainly will not!' The mere thought gave her hysterics.

His eyebrows shot together in a black bar of disapproval.

'Remember what happened before,' he flung at her, and got up to stare out at the view.

She eyed the tension in his shoulders, her uneasiness mounting. 'Look, Gareth, have you really driven all the way to Cardiff just to tell me not to go to Montedaluca?'

'Yes,' he said baldly, and spun round to yank her up into his arms, his mouth on hers with an urgency that felt so wrong her stomach churned.

In utter panic Alicia pushed at him, pummelling his shoulders. 'Stop it!' She wrenched away, gasping for breath. 'What on earth do you think you're doing? That's not who we are, Gareth.'

'It's who I am,' he said hoarsely. 'I want you. I *love* you, Alicia.'

'Don't. Please,' she begged.

'Surely you knew?' he said, in a pleading tone so unlike him she shook her head miserably.

'I had no idea.'

'I could make you love me!' He reached for her again, but she dodged away, fending him off with shaking hands.

'I do love you, Gareth, and I always will—but purely as a brother. Never anything else. Ever.' For the first time in her life, Alicia realised she felt a little wary of him. He was a big man, with the powerful build of a rugby No. 8. There would be nothing she could do, physically, to *make* him go. What if he refused to leave?

She waited, trembling, as Gareth stood poised like a predator about to pounce, then abruptly the tension drained out of his body; he drew in a deep, shuddering breath and raked a hand through his dark hair.

'You know damned well that I'm not your brother! And, believe me, I won't give up, *cariad*. In time I'll make you see that we could be good together.'

'Not this way!' She shook her head vehemently. 'That's never going to happen, Gareth.'

He took her hand, his eyes full of sudden remorse. 'You're shaking!'

'You frightened me,' she said nervously.

'I'm sorry—I would never hurt you, Lally.' He squeezed her hand gently. 'But listen to me. If you really must go back to that blasted place, be careful. Please.'

She tried to smile. 'Of course I will.'

'If da Luca harms one hair of your head, I'll beat his pretty face to a pulp,' he warned. 'Pass on the message.'

'I think he's got that particular message already,' Alicia assured him, so weak with relief when Gareth made for the door her knees were knocking.

'The parents are still in Hay, and Megan doesn't know I'm here,' he said, his eyes sliding away from hers as she saw him out. 'Don't tell them—any of it—please.'

'I won't. Promise. Where are you going now?'

'Do you care?' he said morosely.

'Of course I care. Where will you spend the night?'

His mouth twisted. 'I take it you're not offering to put me up?'

'Afraid not.'

'Then I'll beg a night on a sofa from one of the old gang.' He touched a hand to her cheek. 'Goodnight, Lally. And remember what I said.'

As if she was likely to forget! 'I will. Goodnight, Gareth.'

After he'd gone Alicia collapsed in her chair, heart pounding against the arms she hugged across her chest. Had she been the only one blind all this time? This was one question she could never ask Megan. But Bron would know.

'Mother,' she said, when Bronwen Hughes answered the phone. 'I've had a horrible shock.'

'Oh, good heavens—what *now*?'

Alicia gave her mother every detail of Gareth's visit.

'Just a minute,' said Bron, sighing. 'I need a word with George. I'll ring you back.'

Alicia waited on tenterhooks, then snatched up the phone when it rang. 'I need help, Bron. What can I do about this?'

'George has an early round of golf in the morning, so I'll drive in to see you soon after nine.'

'I'll save you the drive and come to you.'

'No, darling. I'd rather come there. Make sure you've got some good strong coffee while we sort this out.'

After a virtually sleepless night Alicia opened the door to her mother next morning, eyeing her in concern.

'You look tired, Bron,' she said in remorse as she kissed her. 'I'll get the coffee.'

Her mother sank down on the sofa, eyeing her searchingly. 'You don't look too good yourself.'

'Really bad night. Did George think it odd that you were coming to see me again today?'

'No, because I told him why. Besides, he knows I'm only too happy to spend time with you any chance I get.' Bron accepted a cup of coffee gratefully, and drank some of it down.

Alicia pulled her chair nearer. 'Right. Let's get to the point. What in heaven's name do I do about Gareth? Did you have any idea how he felt about me?'

'Once you hit your teens, yes. It worried me to death. He would have been so wrong for you. Getting you away from Gareth was partly why I gave in so easily when you wanted to get married straight from school. I felt safe for the first time in years.'

'Safe?'

'Because you would be married to a man who not only adored you but could give you the security I'd always lacked. The spectre of what happened to me hung over me all my life until I met George. All the time you were growing up, I worried that the same thing might happen to you. Which is why I was so protective and sent you off to the convent to be educated. Fortunately Eira and Huw were happy for Megan to go there too, so it worked well. But now it's time I told you what did happen to me.' Bron took in a deep breath.

Alicia sat forward, suddenly tense.

'First I need to make it clear that I would do anything to keep Eira and Huw from being hurt. So, to show you why, I'll start with what happened when my mother died,' began Bron. 'Mother had never even been ill, like my father. So it was a huge shock when I was told that she'd suffered a major heart attack and all attempts to resuscitate her had failed.'

Alicia's heart contracted. 'And there you were, all alone and only eighteen years old!'

'Except for Eira and Huw.' Bron sighed. 'Mother died just before Christmas, which made it all the worse. When I got back to college afterwards, I was still grieving. A maths lecturer found me in tears in the library while I was doing some research, and when I explained why he took me to his study for a glass of sherry, and mopped me up when I burst into tears again. He was young, and new to the faculty, and hadn't a clue what to do with me, poor man, so he gave me another sherry—bad move. I'd never drunk the stuff before, so the second glass sent me haywire. When he gave me a kindly hug, my response was so uninhibited— Well, I don't have to draw pictures, do I?'

Alicia shook her head. 'So what happened afterwards?'

Bron smiled ruefully. 'I don't know who was more appalled—him or me. He apologised profusely, but I assured him it was as much my fault as his and ran home, thanking my lucky stars that he wasn't one of my tutors. He got married a few weeks later, about which time it finally dawned on me that I was pregnant. So you can understand that there was no way I could ruin the man's life—not to mention his bride's—with my happy news.'

'Oh, Bron!' Alicia went down on her knees beside her mother and clasped her hands. 'Did you tell anybody at all?'

'Only George, when he asked me to marry him,' Bron took in a deep, unsteady breath. 'To my relief he agreed that I did the right thing. But he's always maintained that you deserve the truth.'

Alicia managed a shaky smile. 'At least you've put one of my fears to rest—I'm not the result of an attack or something.'

'God! Is that what you thought? I'm sorry, darling.' Bron shuddered. 'To go on with my tale of woe, I was all for moving out because I was pregnant, but neither Eira nor Huw would hear of it. They were just marvellous. They never badgered me to name the father, and supported my decision to keep my baby. It was even their idea that Eira act as child minder for you so I could carry on at university.' She paused, her hands tightening on Alicia's. 'I owe both of them so much that I'd do anything in my power not to hurt them, or Gareth either. I'm very fond of him. Which means we've got to clear this business up so that his pride is salvaged and his parents never know about it.'

Alicia shivered. 'That's why I got on to you straight away for help.'

'In my opinion, the best way to nip the problem in the bud is to acquire a lover asap,' said Bron, surprising her daughter not a little. 'What about this Jason you've been seeing?'

'No good—he's history. But, before we get into all that, tell me something I've always wanted to know—do I look like my biological father?'

'Nothing at all! He had dark hair and blue eyes.' Bron smiled shakily. 'I was so delighted when my little copper top arrived. Your eyes are dark like mine, but otherwise you follow my grand-mother, freckles, dimples and all. So in grateful tribute to her genes, I named you for her.'

'Thank you, Great-grandma!' Alicia jumped up and went off to make more coffee. 'So, back to the Gareth problem. I don't happen to have a handy lover hanging about.'

'You have a husband.'

Alicia spun round to glare at her parent. 'Don't go there, Mother.'

Bron shrugged. 'I'm just saying that it might do some good if Gareth *thought* you were back with Francesco.'

'Not for Francesco, though.' Alicia chuckled evilly. 'Gareth promised to rearrange his pretty face.'

Bron smiled. 'I'm sure Francesco would handle himself well enough if it ever came to that. He was a rugby player too, remember.'

'How could I ever forget?'

'Do you still have his action photograph?'

'No,' lied Alicia. Not even to her mother would she admit that she hadn't been able to throw it away.

'Talking of Francesco, let me drive you to the airport on Tuesday,' offered Bron.

'That's sweet of you, but no need. The air ticket came with a note saying a car will pick me up on Tuesday.'

'Goodness! Francesco's obviously determined to make sure you get to Montedaluca.'

Alicia smiled sardonically. 'Of course he is. Until I sign whatever legal papers are necessary, he can't get on with a divorce and marry again.'

Bron looked thoughtful. 'Is that what he wants?'

'He hasn't said it in so many words, but it must be what he has in mind.'

'And, after the divorce, will *you* think about marrying again, darling?'

Alicia shrugged. 'Who knows? Right now I like my life just the way it is.'

CHAPTER SIX

FRANCESCO paced the entrance hall at Galileo Galilei airport in Pisa, cursing himself for arriving so early. It would be a long, fraught wait before he knew whether Alicia had actually boarded the plane in the UK. Ignoring the constant ebb and flow of passengers around him, he thought, as he had done almost constantly since, of Alicia in their last meeting at her apartment. In her stark black, self-contained and sophisticated, she had looked so different from the shy, appealing girl he had fallen in love with in Florence. There had been no sign of her enchanting dimples, nor the freckles she had once hated so much.

Once he had finally ceased bombarding Bronwen Cross with demands to see his wife, his da Luca pride had ordered him to forget Alicia, to put her out of his mind and his life. And in minor ways he had succeeded. There were many beautiful women in Tuscany, and, with the safety net of an estranged wife to protect him from any possibility of commitment, he had allowed more than one of them to soothe the pride scarred by his bride's desertion.

But life had taken a sudden, different turn with the death of his mother. This had not only brought him grief, but the surprise of the legacy left to her daughter-in-law. The ticket for the Italy v Wales match had arrived soon afterwards, with an invitation to lunch with some old rugby friends in Cardiff before the match, and he had taken this as a sign that fate was urging him to contact

Alicia. And when he had come face to face with her he had been stunned by the change in her, amazed that a woman so desirable had no man in her life urging her to get a divorce. His jaw tightened. From that first moment the mere thought of other men in her life had enraged him. At the party he had exerted much self-control to hide his objection to the male attention Alicia had attracted in that seductive little dress.

Francesco checked the arrivals board again, and swore when he saw that the plane was delayed. He began his restless pacing again, thinking back to the halcyon days in Florence, when he had fallen deeper in love by the day with the shy young woman who for him had been the epitome of innocence and purity. His mother had long been urging him to marry, and in contrast to the more mature charms of the women he'd known at the time an innocent, virgin bride had strongly appealed to the primitive instincts concealed by the polished façade Francesco da Luca presented to the world.

His eyes softened. Alicia had been the quintessential virgin bride. The picture of her was as clear in his mind now as it had been when she walked down the aisle of the *cattedrale* on the arm of proud Huw Davies. In a slim column of satin, with the creamy tint of the roses she carried, the fiery gleam of her hair hidden by a froth of veil, Alicia had looked as pure and pale as one of the lilies wreathing the altar rail. Her ice-cold hand had trembled in his as she made her responses in a breathless little voice. She had been so obviously overwhelmed by the long nuptial-mass, and the even longer wedding feast that followed at the *Castello*, that he had allowed his exhausted bride to sleep in peace in his bed that night with no more than a kiss.

How nobly restrained he had been, he thought savagely. He had forced himself to wait for their true consummation until they reached the bridal suite of the hotel in Paris chosen for their honeymoon. As soon as they were alone, even though it was only late afternoon, he had seized his little bride so passionately she had been as eager as he to celebrate their marriage there and then.

Francesco clenched his teeth at the memory of his anticipation when Alicia so sweetly coaxed him to wait a little while she got ready for him in their bedroom. He had resolved to take his time, to be gentle, slow, lead her step by step to the joy to be found between a man and a woman. But when she finally opened the door he had stared at her in horror.

She had let her curls loose in a wild aureole, and painted her face so thickly with cosmetics she was almost unrecognisable as his shy little Alicia. The vulgar black garment she wore barely covered her breasts, and ended only just below the apex of her thighs, the transparent chiffon showing all too plainly that she had even reddened her nipples. For a moment he had been speechless at the sight of his bride decked out like a whore—then, when the words came tumbling out at last in a harsh torrent of displeasure, his command of English had failed him in places. But by the stricken look on Alicia's face she had understood every word, most of all the snarled *puttana*. With the twenty-twenty vision of hindsight he could see now that in his disgust and rampant sexual frustration he had been unforgivably cruel as he ordered his sobbing bride to scrub herself clean. He had stormed out of the room and down to the bar to wait until he'd calmed down. But, though remorse had soon replaced his anger, when he returned to their suite Alicia had vanished. She had taken none of the new luggage, and, instead of a note, as a graphic farewell message her wedding ring lay on the heap of tawdry black chiffon, along with the heirloom da Luca betrothal ring handed over by his mother.

Dio, how frantic he had been! Francesco felt an icy shiver even now as he remembered his frenzied appeals to the hotel manager, who had eventually learned that a young girl with a back pack had been seen entering a car outside the portico of the hotel. Francesco's phone had rung soon afterwards, but his relief at hearing Alicia's voice had been so intense he'd barely understood what the cold little voice was saying until it was too late.

'I've taken my disgusting self out of your sight *and* your life forever. Goodbye.'

'*Alicia—*' But she had switched off her phone. He had immediately rung Bronwen Cross, praying she was already back in Blake Street after the flight home that morning, but his relief was short-lived when she answered. She had already heard briefly from Alicia, and refused to say another word until her daughter arrived home to say exactly why she'd run away. His incensed mother-in-law relented enough to promise a phone call as soon as Alicia got back, and early next morning, after a night of sleepless misery, Francesco received the call as promised. Alicia, her mother informed him with fierce hostility, was safe at home but in a state of deep distress.

'I don't know what unspeakable thing you did to make her run away, Francesco, because she won't tell me. But on one subject she was very explicit—she refuses to see or speak to you again. Ever.'

Francesco came back to the present with a jolt when he saw Alicia's flight appear on the monitor. He waited with mounting impatience until he spotted a bright head among the stream of disembarking passengers from the UK, and let out the breath he'd been unaware he was holding. She was here! But Alicia, casual in jeans and linen jacket, was not alone.

'No, really, thank you just the same,' Francesco heard her say to the man with her. 'Please give me my bag. I can manage now.'

He strode forward to claim her with a kiss on each cheek. '*Com' esta, carissima?* You had a good flight?'

'Francesco!' She smiled at him in such relief her dimples came into play, and just seeing them again evoked such a visceral rush of response he wanted to seize her in his arms and kiss her senseless. 'Will you relieve this kind gentleman of my luggage?' she asked.

'With pleasure.' He took the bag the man held out and smiled graciously. '*Mille grazie;* how kind of you to assist my wife.'

The man backed away, crestfallen. 'No problem—only too glad to help.'

'Thank you so much,' said Alicia sweetly. 'Goodbye.'

The greetings were over, and they were in the car speeding along the express route to Florence before Francesco spoke his mind.

'So, Alicia, you came.'

'I said I would.'

'You look most charming, but a little tired. Have you been working hard?'

'No more than usual.'

'While you are here you must rest.'

'I won't be staying long enough for that,' she said quickly. Though now she was actually here in the sunshine of Tuscany her urgency to leave it right away was fading fast.

'I will try to change your mind,' said Francesco, in a tone which won him a suspicious look.

'Could I ask a favour, Francesco?' she said, surprising him.

'Of course.'

'Could we make a stop somewhere on the way to Montedaluca so I can change my clothes and tidy myself up?' She smiled wryly. 'In the circumstances, I'd rather not arrive in jeans.'

'Even though you look so delightful in them?'

She turned away, her face warm. 'Even so.'

'*Va bene.* Because I have a suggestion to make.'

'What is it?'

'*Il notaio* who is handling the will is not available until Thursday, therefore we can make this stop you desire in Florence and stay the night there before we travel on to Montedaluca.' He slanted a wary look at her. 'The apartment has two bedrooms.'

Instead of the instant refusal he expected, Alicia surprised him by giving the suggestion some thought.

'Couldn't the lawyer make it any earlier?' she asked after a while. Bedrooms aside, she found she was not at all averse to seeing Florence again if it meant putting off the visit to Montedaluca a bit longer.

'Unfortunately for you he cannot, Alicia. But for me this is good fortune, yes?'

'I don't know. Is it?' She eyed his profile narrowly. 'I noticed you referred to me as your wife back there.'

'It most efficiently relieved you of your companion.' He shot a gleaming look at her. 'Or did you not desire that?'

'Of course I did. The man sat by me on the plane and talked to me all the way, even suggested meeting in Florence for a meal. I couldn't get rid of him.'

'Why not tell him your husband was meeting you at the airport?'

She shrugged. 'I don't think of you as my husband, Francesco. Besides, you could have been sending a driver to pick me up, as you did in Cardiff. Thank you for that, by the way,' she added.

'It was my pleasure. But, Alicia, surely you knew I would come to meet you myself?' He touched a hand to hers.

Since Francesco was a fast driver, and she disliked travelling on motorways of any kind, British or Italian, Alicia begged him to keep both hands on the wheel and leave any further conversation until they arrived.

'*Scusi*. I had forgotten you are a nervous traveller!'

'Only as a passenger these days—I'm perfectly happy when I'm in the driving seat.'

Francesco did as she asked, and said no more for the remainder of the journey, while Alicia wondered if she was mad to even consider staying in Florence overnight with Francesco. But she wanted to. It was useless trying to delude herself that she felt nothing for him. From the moment of seeing him again at the Millennium Stadium, it had been obvious that whatever had attracted her in the first place was not only still alive and well but was something she had never found in any other man. And probably never would. Fool, she told herself angrily. Get a life, Alicia Cross. One without the spectre of Francesco da Luca hanging over it. But first, said a sly little voice in her mind, she might as well take advantage of this unexpected interlude.

She was deeply thankful when they arrived in the cool, raftered apartment at last, and the moment Francesco ushered her inside she made straight for the window in the main room to look down on the thronged Piazza dei Signoria.

'Perseus is still there,' Francesco assured her. 'Come, I will take your suitcase to your room. After you unpack would you like tea?'

'Yes, please.' She followed him into a bedroom and halted, frowning. 'This is obviously yours, Francesco. Can't I just use the other room rather than put you out?'

'No. Here you have your own bathroom, also the better view.' He moved closer and touched a strand of escaping hair. 'And you like views, Alicia, no?'

'Yes.' She tensed, very much aware that they were alone in Francesco's bedroom, and he was looking at her with those long-lashed eyes that were such an improbable colour she had wondered at first if he wore tinted lenses. They had once made her heart hammer in her chest. And infuriatingly still did. This was a mistake. She should have insisted they go straight to Montedaluca. 'Tea sounds wonderful,' she said brightly. 'But could I have a shower first?'

'Of course. You may have whatever you wish, Alicia,' he assured her, and left her alone with the view.

There was not much to unpack for an overnight stay, but it took longer than it should have when Alicia found her clothes had to share space with some of Francesco's in a big armoire that, unlike the modern furniture in the living room, was a carved, antique piece of great beauty. In the bathroom it felt even more intimate to arrange her toilet articles alongside the Aqua di Parma items Francesco had always used. It was that same subtle, familiar fragrance that had struck her dumb in the taxi to her flat after the party.

She stripped off her T-shirt and jeans, wound a towel round her hair and showered quickly, then dried off at top speed and put on the fresh clothes she'd taken with her into the bathroom rather than help herself to Francesco's towelling robe or, worse, venture out into the bedroom wearing only a towel. She made a few swift repairs, then joined Francesco in the living room, expecting to find a tea tray ready for her.

'I thought you might like to go down to Rivoire for the tea,' he said, surprising her. He surveyed her appearance with such pleasure Alicia was grateful, not for the first time, for her mother's faultless taste. Her beautifully cut fawn linen trousers and ivory silk shirt had cost a lot, but by the look in Francesco's eyes it had been money well spent.

'You look most elegant, Alicia,' he commented. 'But tell me— what has happened to your freckles?'

She smiled wryly. 'Nothing, unfortunately. They're hiding behind concealing cream worth every penny of the fortune I pay for it.'

'I miss them,' he said simply as they went down in the lift. 'And until you smiled at me so radiantly at the airport I had missed your dimples also.'

'I was very relieved to see you,' she admitted as they emerged into the soft evening sunshine. 'That man was such a nuisance.'

'If he made you smile at me I am grateful to him.' Francesco led her to a table outside the café of their first meeting and held out a chair for her. 'The sun is not fierce now, *carina*, so you need have no worry for your freckles.'

It wasn't her freckles she was worried about. Alicia eyed him moodily as he gave their order to the waiter.

'What is troubling you?' Francesco demanded as he turned back to her. 'You are frowning.'

She met his eyes frankly. 'It occurs to me that staying here at the apartment with you might be looked on as co-habiting, and affect the divorce in some way. In which case I'd rather we went straight to Montedaluca tonight.'

'You are expected there tomorrow. I did not mention that you were arriving at Pisa today. No one knows you are here at the *appartamento*.' His eyes locked with hers. 'But this obviously worries you. Are you are in such a hurry for a divorce?'

'None at all,' she said impatiently. 'You're the one who wants the divorce, not me.'

Francesco shook his head. 'I have no desire for a divorce either. There are times when it is most convenient to have a wife in the background.'

Alicia raised a cynical eyebrow. 'So you can have the bun without the penny!'

He frowned. 'I do not understand, *cara*.'

'Oh yes, you do, Francesco! If your current squeeze starts thinking about marriage you just give her a sad, regretful reminder about a wife who won't set you free.'

'Squeeze?'

'Girlfriend.'

'Ah.' He nodded, lips twitching. 'It is a very useful arrangement, no? Does it also work well for you?'

There was a pause while they were served with tea and coffee. Once they were alone again Alicia sipped some of the tea before she answered Francesco's question.

'I avoid the subject, but if pushed I say something vague about divorce. I never mention you,' she added flatly.

He shot her a narrowed look. 'I am the skeleton in the cupboard?'

'You bet you are.'

Francesco downed his espresso quickly. 'But there *are* people who know about me.'

'If you mean Megan, Rhys and the rest of the Davies clan, of course none of them would ever say a word.' Alicia looked at him levelly. 'You are not a popular subject of conversation in my family.'

'Because they think I was cruel to you?'

'You were!'

Francesco's eyes held hers. 'And if I could erase the memory of my words from your mind I would do it, no matter what the cost.'

'Too late now,' she said dismissively, then eyed him in dawning suspicion. 'Hold *on*. If you're not in a hurry for a divorce, Francesco, why were you so insistent on getting me back here? I thought I had to sign documents of some kind.'

'*Davverro*. But only those documents which refer to my mother's will.'

She frowned. 'Is this true? About the divorce, I mean?'

'Yes.' He leaned back in his chair with the negligent grace that was so much part of him. 'Because I am Catholic.'

'How could I forget?' she said acidly.

'Let me speak, *per favore*. I do not find it easy to explain this,' he said, his eyes reproachful. 'It is sometimes difficult for me in English.'

'You know very well that your English is excellent. But I'm listening, so do go on.'

'*Grazie*. Even though times have changed very much in Italy, as in the rest of the world, I, personally, find the prospect of divorce very difficult.' He shrugged. 'But if you wish for one I will not contest it, Alicia. Ask Huw Davies to help you.'

She stared at him blankly. 'But I thought you wanted to marry again, to get heirs for Montedaluca.'

'If I am ever fortunate enough to have a child,' he said coldly, 'I shall be delighted because I have a son or a daughter, not because I have fathered an heir for Montedaluca.'

Alicia's eyes flashed. 'My deepest apologies, *Signor Conte*. I was given to understand very clearly that my duty as your wife was to provide Montedaluca with an heir right away.'

For a moment their table was a small oasis of silence in the noise and bustle of the *piazza*. 'My mother made many mistakes with you,' said Francesco at last, and sighed deeply. 'It is a miracle that you did not run away before the wedding, not after it. Did you ever consider this, Alicia?'

'Every day.'

'Yet you did not. Why?'

Her eyes met his. 'I was madly in love with you, Francesco. Though right from day one in Montedaluca I began to have doubts about rushing into marriage so quickly. But in the end I just couldn't bring myself to back out when your mother had worked so hard on all the preparations. I didn't have the bottle.'

'Bottle?'

'Courage.' She smiled ruefully. 'I was only a teenager, remember. And a very unsophisticated one, compared to the normal variety.'

'You were enchanting. That is why I could not understand—' He stopped, shrugging. 'It is pointless to spend time in regrets.

Instead let us try to enjoy this brief time we have together. Or,' he added, looking into her eyes, 'do you still hate me too much for that, Alicia?'

She turned away sharply and kept her eyes on the scene before her as it began to grow dark. The lights had come on in the crowded *piazza*. Neptune glistened among his nymphs, and David and Perseus held sway in their spotlights as Florence got ready to enjoy the evening. So she might as well do the same. Given the choice she wouldn't have come back to Florence again to revive memories better left forgotten. But now she was here it would be silly to pretend that her surroundings failed to cast at least some of their original spell.

She turned to face him. 'I don't hate you, Francesco.' Which was the truth. Her feelings had begun to change the instant she'd learned that he actually had come to Cardiff to look for her. Or even before that, when she first laid eyes on him again. Otherwise she would have refused to make the trip, no matter what legalities demanded it. 'It was a good idea to break the journey here in Florence. I'll be able to go on to Montedaluca in a far better frame of mind.'

Francesco touched her hand fleetingly. 'I am happy that you do not hate me, Alicia.'

'I did for quite a long time, because quite apart from anything else I thought you were glad to get rid of me. There was no way I could tell Bron what really happened, so she pictured a far worse scenario, sent you and the *contessa* away and swore the others to silence about your visit.'

'I am relieved,' he said somberly, 'that she knows I did not beat you—or worse.'

'No. You just broke my heart.' Alicia smiled bleakly. 'But, as I told you before, it mended. Eventually.'

They sat in silence again for a while. 'If it is of any comfort to you, Alicia,' said Francesco softly, 'my heart suffered also.'

She thought about it, then nodded. 'It is, a little. Just knowing that you and the *contessa* came to find me is a comfort too. It would have been an even bigger one if I'd known at the time. But let's not dwell on the past any more, Francesco.'

'*Va bene*,' he said promptly. 'Since we are together at last, in the place where we first met, I must take advantage of this. Who knows when it will happen again?'

'True.'

'So, instead of sad things, let us think of dinner.'

She laughed. 'Spoken like a true Italian! Where are we eating?'

Francesco's face took on the arrested expression she'd first seen long ago, right here at a table at the Caffe Rivoire. 'It is so good to hear you laugh, Alicia.' He rose to his feet. 'Where would you like to eat?'

'How about the restaurant with the wonderful frescoes?'

'An excellent choice.'

Alicia wasn't so sure about that as they strolled to Santa Croce later. Revisiting the scene of their first dinner together was a bit rash under the circumstances. And the restaurant couldn't possibly be as magical as she remembered it. But this was a special occasion, and both of them were dressed for it. Francesco was wearing a suit very much like the one worn on that first evening, but the dress Bron had bought her to impress everyone at Montedaluca was very different from the simple little shift worn on her eighteenth birthday. It was so much warmer here than at home; it was the perfect evening for sleeveless, bias-cut layers of cotton voile in a muted shade of almost-pink called 'ashes of roses'. And for once Alicia had released her curls from their knot, and caught them back with a silver filigree clasp at the nape of her neck.

'You look very beautiful,' said Francesco. 'Did your mother make that dress?'

'No. But she paid for it.' Alicia smiled up at him. 'Bron does very little actual sewing these days. When she married George she hired two managers, one for the shop and the other for the actual dress-making studio. She keeps an executive eye on both, and even lends a hand when things get busy. But now and again, if a friend pleads on behalf of a daughter, Bron still makes the occasional wedding dress herself.'

'The gown she made for you was perfection.'

'What happened to it?'

'It is stored away very carefully at the *castello*.' He arched an eyebrow. 'Since it is your mother's work, would you like to have it back?'

'If you want me to take it back, I will,' she said carefully.

He shook his head. 'I would like very much to keep it, as a *ricordo* of what might have been, Alicia.'

'Ricordo?'

He thought for a moment. 'Keepsake—is that right?'

She nodded, so surprised to find a lump in her throat she resorted to flippancy. 'Maybe you could recycle it for my successor.'

He looked down his aquiline da Luca nose. 'Even if I could find a lady slender enough to wear it, I would never suggest such a thing.'

When they reached the *palazzo* which housed the restaurant it was a bittersweet experience to mount the dais at the back again, and sit at one of the tables for two. Alicia gazed nostalgically at the fresco of knights in the flickering candlelight, and sighed a little. The magic was still there. In spades.

'You were lucky to get a table like this at such short notice,' she commented.

'I had already reserved it,' he said casually as a waiter arrived with menus.

By the time they were left alone to make their choices some of Alicia's irritation at his high-handedness had subsided. 'How did you know I'd ask to come here again?'

Francesco shrugged. 'I did not. I made the reservation because at this time of year it cannot be done at the last minute.'

'And if I'd chosen to go elsewhere?'

'There are many restaurants in Florence, *cara*, and most of them can provide a table at short notice, even this one. Though not at one of these special tables up here. What would you like to eat?' he added.

She studied the menu. 'I think I fancy the roast pork with rosemary.'

'I shall join you.' Francesco raised an eyebrow and the wine waiter instantly materialised at his elbow. 'We shall drink some Rosso di Montedaluca with it.'

Even if the food had not been delicious, the surroundings, as before, were enough to put Alicia in a mood as mellow as the wine she was served. 'I wondered if this place could possibly be as magical as I remembered, Francesco, but it is.'

'I have never been back since your birthday dinner here,' he said, surprising her.

'Why not?'

'Surely that is obvious? After you left me it would have been too painful.' His eyes met hers, their glitter intensified by the candle flames. 'Tonight it is not painful, just unbelievable. I did not expect—or even hope—to face you over a dinner table again, Alicia.'

'I didn't, either.' She smiled suddenly. 'How civilised we are.'

His eyes darkened. 'You have attracted too much attention for me to feel civilised.'

'Have I?' she said, surprised, and tried to peer beyond the circle of light that enclosed them.

'There were many men's eyes on you as we walked to our table.'

'How flattering.'

'Such appreciation cannot be unusual for you, Alicia, when you work amongst rugby players!'

'The ones I know give me no trouble at all—perfect gentlemen every one of them. But then,' she added sweetly, 'I'm talking about my fellow countrymen.'

'You must surely have met players from other countries.'

'Of course I have. Lots. In fact, I've been seeing one of them recently. Maybe you've heard of him—Jason Forrester, English ex-Saracens player?'

'No, I have not.' Francesco drained his glass. 'He is your lover?'

'Not any more.' *Or ever.* 'Due to our respective careers it was so difficult to arrange time together; he began hinting at a more permanent relationship, so I nipped it in the bud.'

'*Cosa?*'

'I ended it.'

'Why?'

'As I keep saying, marriage—or even a committed relationship—just doesn't appeal to me.'

Francesco surveyed her moodily for a while. 'Does a *dolce* appeal to you, Alicia?' he said eventually.

She shook her head. 'But it was a delicious meal. Thank you for bringing me here again.'

'It was my great pleasure,' he responded, equally formal.

They walked back in silence Alicia found hard to break. Yet they'd been enjoying the evening together until her remark about Jason had put Francesco into a bad mood. Could he really resent someone he'd never met? When they reached the Piazza della Signoria she felt tired as they went up in the lift to Francesco's apartment; no surprise there. Since the shock of Gareth's visit she'd hardly slept. The men in her life were giving her a lot of hassle at the moment. Because since they'd met up again Francesco da Luca was very definitely in her life again. It was pointless trying to pretend otherwise.

Once they were inside the apartment, Francesco spoke at last. 'Would you like a drink, or tea or coffee, Alicia?'

She stifled a yawn, wanting nothing more than bed and oblivion for a few hours. 'No thanks, Francesco.' She smiled a little. 'The insomnia of the past week is catching up with me. I desperately need some sleep.'

His eyes softened. 'I told Giacomo we would arrive in Montedaluca for lunch tomorrow, so we need not start early. Sleep as long as you like.'

'Thank you. Good night.'

'*Buona notte*, Alicia.' He smiled at last, and she smiled back, allowing her dimples to come into play as she left him.

Thankful that the going-to-bed bit had passed off reasonably well, Alicia's tension lessened as she closed the bedroom door behind her. She hung her dress away, and after a short session in the bathroom stretched out with a sigh under the covers in Francesco's beautiful antique bed. A good thing Gareth didn't know where she was tonight, was her last thought as she went to sleep.

CHAPTER SEVEN

STRONG arms were crushing the life out of her. At last a relentless, devouring mouth lifted from hers long enough for Alicia to scream in panic, and she woke up with a start as the light went on and Francesco hurtled into the room, wild-eyed, shrugging into a dressing gown as he ran.

'Sorry. I—had—a nightmare,' she gasped, shivering so violently he sat on the edge of the bed and pulled her up into his arms.

'*Gran Dio*, Alicia,' he said hoarsely, 'You gave me the heart attack.'

'My heart's not so good, either,' she panted against his chest.

He rubbed his chin over her sweat-soaked curls as his heartbeat slowed. 'What was this dream?' he demanded.

'I can't remember,' she lied.

Francesco put her away from him, his eyes widening in consternation. '*Santo cielo*, you are soaked—also the sheets.' He released her and made for the bathroom. He returned with his towelling robe. 'Put this on. I will find more sheets.'

'I need a shower,' she said, teeth chattering.

'Later, *cara*. Sit now while I fetch the linen. I shall be quick,' he promised.

Alicia stripped off her camisole and briefs and pulled on the robe that smelled of Francesco. She thought about stripping the bed, but her hands were shaking too much. What an idiot for thinking about Gareth as she got into bed! No wonder she'd had a nightmare and given Francesco the fright of his life. She sat down in the chair beside the small table under the windows, pushing her sodden hair back from her face, and smiled in remorse as Francesco came back with an armful of bed linen.

'Sorry I gave you such a shock. I shouldn't have had that second glass of wine.'

'I do not think it was the wine,' he said grimly, and began to strip the bed. 'You were screaming at Gareth—begging him to stop.'

She covered her shudder with a shrug. 'It was just a dream, Francesco.'

'A dream that drenches you with terror? I think not,' he said scornfully, working with an efficiency that surprised Alicia. She had never pictured the Conte da Luca doing anything so menial. 'Have you had the dream before?'

She nodded unwillingly. 'But only lately.'

'So lately something has happened to cause this.' He put out a hand to touch her hair. 'It is still damp, *carina*. Go and have your shower. Afterwards would you like tea or a cold drink?'

'Something cold, please.'

When Alicia emerged from the bathroom with her own dressing gown tied securely over fresh night things, the bed was immaculate again. She detangled wet strands of hair with a comb, hoping her taming solution would do its thing quickly, then smiled ruefully as she heard Francesco's discreet knock on his own bedroom door.

'Come in.'

He came in with a tray of drinks, eyeing her closely. 'You are better now?'

'Much better. Sorry to make such a fuss.'

He set the tray down on the small table beside her. 'It is obvious that something caused such a dream, Alicia. You have quarrelled with Gareth?'

'Not quarrelled, exactly,' she said carefully. 'We had a mis-understanding.'

'When?'

'Recently. But it's sorted now.' At least she hoped it was.

'*Bene*. If you will get into bed I shall give you your drink.'

'I'll just sit in the chair for a bit while my hair dries. I'd hate to spoil all your good work with the bed.' She sat down, deliberately bringing her dimples into play as she smiled at him. 'I'm impressed, Francesco.'

'Because I can make a bed?' He grinned, looking suddenly like the young Francesco of the action photograph. 'You think I am not capable of such things?'

'I'm sure you're capable of a great many things, Francesco, but you and household chores are an unlikely combination.'

He handed her an ice-filled glass of orange juice. 'At the *castello* I do none of these things, but here in my *appartamento* I live my other life, with no servants but more freedom. It is still my bolt hole, Alicia.'

'I just can't picture you dusting and sweeping.'

'The caretaker's wife does that for me. But,' he added virtuously, 'I change my bed myself.'

Alicia laughed, her eyes dancing. 'So you're not really domesticated at all.'

'You require such skill from the men in your life?'

'It's not mandatory. But these days so many women juggle careers with families that a lot of men, even hunky rugby players, are more domesticated than they used to be. Which is only fair.'

'*Davverro*.' Francesco sat on the edge of bed. 'Do you wish to do such juggling with your life, Alicia?'

'At the moment my job is more than enough for me.' She finished her drink and put the glass on the tray. 'Thank you. That was exactly what I needed.'

'You are feeling better now?'

'Yes.'

'Then *per favore*, Alicia,' he said urgently, 'tell me about this misunderstanding with Gareth that gives you nightmares. He is not pleased about your return to Montedaluca?'

She pulled a face. 'No, he most certainly isn't. He made a special trip to ask—beg—me not to come.'

Francesco's mouth tightened. 'He hates me, no? And he is crazy about you, Alicia. When you left me I was sure he would persuade you to marry him.'

Her eyes widened. '*Were* you? I never had the slightest idea—' She stopped, shivering, and Francesco took a blanket from the chest at the foot of the bed and tucked it around her.

'You are cold. It is the reaction,' he said, and resumed his seat on the edge of the bed. 'But I am amazed that you did not know how Gareth felt about you.'

She shook her head. 'To me he was always just as much my brother as Megan's.'

'But he does not think of you as his sister.'

'Apparently not.'

There was silence for a moment, then Francesco sent her pulse into orbit. 'After you divorce me will you marry him?' He eyed her in consternation as her face whitened, and slid to his knees beside her to take her hand. 'You feel ill? What is wrong, *tesoro*?'

Alicia grasped his hand tightly, glad of the hard, warm contact.

'If there is something I can do tell me,' he ordered. 'Anything to take that look from your eyes, Alicia. You are worrying me.'

She thought long and hard, and at last looked into the brilliant, watchful eyes, her decision made. 'Francesco, I am going to trust you with a secret you must swear never to tell anyone.'

The eyes narrowed. 'You have my word as a da Luca, Alicia. And now you are worrying me even more. It is so very bad, this secret?'

'Perhaps secret is the wrong word. It's more a problem,' she said quietly. 'Do get up, Francesco.'

'I will, because since the rugby my knee gives me the twinges sometimes,' he confessed ruefully. 'But you must not tell, because this is *my* secret. Very bad for my image.'

Alicia managed a smile. 'Disastrous!'

He resumed his place on the edge of the bed. 'That is better.

Take a look at what's on offer at
www.millsandboon.co.uk

⦿ MILLS & BOON®
Pure reading pleasure

My Account / Offer of the Month / Our Authors / Book Club / Contact us

All of the latest books are there **PLUS**

- ⊚ Free Online reads
- ⊚ **Exclusive** offers and competitions
- ⊚ At least **15% discount** on our huge back list
- ⊚ Sign up to our **free monthly eNewsletter**

- ⊚ More info on your **favourite authors**
- ⊚ **Browse the Book** to try before you buy
- ⊚ **eBooks** available for most titles
- ⊚ Join the M&B community and **discuss your favourite books** with other readers

You have a little warmth in your face now. And I am delighted to see your freckles again, *cara*.'

'How you do go on about my freckles!'

'At this moment I am more interested in this secret of yours.' His eyes narrowed again as comprehension dawned. 'Ah! You have finally solved the mystery of your father, no?'

'Yes.' Alicia took in a deep, steadying breath and began to tell him, slowly and carefully, the bare bones of her mother's story. Francesco sat utterly still, listening intently to every word, then slid down to his knees again to take her hand.

'So what is the problem with Gareth?'

Alicia shivered. 'When Gareth came to beg me not to go to Montedaluca he—he tried to make love to me.'

'*Santo cielo*—so this is why you had the nightmare!' Francesco pulled her to her feet. 'Come sit by me on the bed so I can hold your hand.'

Alicia obeyed so reluctantly, Francesco smiled at her sardonically.

'Do not worry. I shall not make Gareth's mistake.'

'Oh, I know that.'

'Do you?'

She nodded. 'Otherwise I wouldn't have agreed to stay here in the apartment with you, Francesco.'

'*Grazie!*' His smile was wry as he took her hand again. 'So what did your mother say when you told her of this love-making?'

'She decided to tell me, at last, who my biological father is to stress how different her life would have been without Eira and Huw's support, not only when she was pregnant, but all the years since. She's desperate to save them pain over this problem with Gareth and me. A problem Bron has always been worried about, apparently.'

'But not you?'

'No, never. Which is why it was such a shock when he kissed me like that.' She felt Francesco tense.

'He did not—hurt you?' he asked carefully.

'No. My problem was trying to hide how much the kiss appalled me.'

'*Dio!* It is an unusual problem. Did your mother give you advice on how to deal with it?'

'She told me to acquire a lover as soon as possible.'

'No!' said Francesco flatly. 'Why a lover when you have a husband? The solution is simple—just tell Gareth that we are together again.'

Alicia turned to look at him. 'He won't believe it.'

'We can very easily make him believe it,' he assured her with supreme confidence. 'We shall simply make it known that we are no longer *separato*.'

She bit her lip. 'I can just imagine his reaction to that! In fact, Gareth was worried that if I went to Montedaluca you might lock me up in your *castello*, where anything might happen, according to him.'

Francesco's eyebrows rose. 'He is a reader of Gothic fiction?'

She grinned at the mere idea. 'No. Rugby biographies are his literature of choice. But where you're concerned he tends to lose his temper too easily. He even threatened to do damage to your pretty face.'

Francesco snorted. 'He can try! But I am serious, Alicia. Your mother's idea is an excellent one. But instead of a lover she can break the news that you are staying here in Montedaluca for a while. With your husband.'

'You mean we pretend for a while until Gareth cools off?'

'*Davverro*. When you go home I shall go with you, and make my peace with your mother. Then Gareth will be convinced that we are reconciled, no?'

'It sounds like a lot of trouble for you,' she said doubtfully.

'Not as much trouble as you once caused me, *sposa mia*!' He eyed her sternly. 'But this time no running away, Alicia. No matter what Gareth believes, I will not keep you in the *castello* against your will. When you wish to finish the pretence, just tell me.'

'All right,' she said, not at all sure what exactly she was

agreeing to. Suddenly everything seemed too much to cope with, and she yawned widely. 'Sorry! These broken nights are putting years on me.'

Francesco shook his head. 'You look no older tonight, *carina*, than you did at eighteen. I am delighted to see your freckles again—forgive me for mentioning these again. I have great fondness for them.' He got up and turned down the covers. 'Now is the time to forget about dark secrets and just sleep. But if you have bad dreams,' he added, 'I shall come to you.'

'Thank you,' she said, fervently hoping the need wouldn't arise.

'Come. Let me take the dressing gown.' He smiled as she shook her head. 'Ah. You are afraid to remove it for fear I take advantage of our new arrangement.'

She made no attempt to deny it. 'Goodnight, Francesco.'

He bent to kiss her cheek. '*Buona notte*, Alicia.'

The moment the door closed behind him she stripped off the dressing gown and slid into the fresh, cool bed with a sigh of relief. But she left the bedside lamp on as her candle against the dark.

Alicia surfaced again to the wonderful smell of coffee and a tap on the door, and shot out of bed to wrap herself in her dressing gown and push her hair behind her ears.

'Come in.'

'*Buongiorno.*' Francesco, hair damp from a shower, smiled as he came in with a tray. 'Did you sleep, Alicia?'

'Good morning. I went out like a light. Unlike this one.' Embarrassed, she switched off the bedside lamp. 'I couldn't cope with the dark last night.'

'It is not surprising.' Francesco put the tray down, eyeing her closely. 'You look better. No more dreams?'

'No. If you give me five minutes to wash and brush my teeth, I'll be with you.'

'Hurry, or I shall eat all the pastries,' he warned.

Alicia rejoined Francesco quickly, growing more conscious by the minute that this visit was proceeding along vastly different lines from the ones she'd intended. For years she had thought of Francesco, when she allowed herself to think of him at all, as the villain of her story. But since they'd met up again his role had begun to change. Considerably.

'What are you thinking?' asked Francesco as he filled the coffee cups.

'That this is not what I expected.'

'This?'

'You and me, together here like old friends, instead of—' She stopped short, biting her lip.

'Enemies.' He seated her in one of the chairs he'd pulled up to the table. 'Perhaps you are now able to think of me without remembering the tragedy of our parting.'

'Tragedy?'

The brilliant eyes held hers. 'When a man causes such hurt to his bride she runs away on their wedding night what else is it? There is some other English word that describes it better?'

Alicia drank some of the heavenly coffee and took a brioche. 'Probably not. But since we're on the subject of our wedding night, Francesco, it's time you knew exactly why I slapped on the make-up and decked myself out in that extraordinary garment. It wasn't my idea. I'd been given precise instructions on how to make myself more alluring for you.' Her mouth twisted. 'But when you saw the result you looked ready to throw up.'

'Throw up?'

'Vomitare?'

He nodded, his eyes narrowed and intent. 'You said instructions—who gave you these?'

Alicia refilled their cups, wondering whether he was up to the truth. But it was time he knew. 'Your mother.'

'Cosa!' Francesco looked as though he'd taken a blow to the stomach. 'My mother told you to paint yourself like a *puttana*?'

'Not personally. She sent Cinzia to me with a gift just before we left the *castello*, with instructions to open it in Paris.' Alicia's mouth twisted. 'I was so pathetically pleased that your mother had given me a present, I even thanked her warmly as we said goodbye. But I was shocked rigid when I opened the package. And absolutely astounded when I read the instructions that went with the nightgown. But, because it was your mother's advice on what my bridegroom would expect, I took it as gospel and followed it to the letter.'

Francesco shook his head vehemently. 'Alicia, it was a mistake. My mother would never give you such a—a garment.'

'I didn't think you would believe me.'

'Did you keep the note?'

Alicia's mouth curled in distaste. 'Are you serious? I flushed it down the lavatory before I ran.'

'I am not surprised.' He frowned. 'By the time I collected my mother to travel to Cardiff to look for you, she had dismissed Cinzia. I was too devastated about you to care, or to ask why.' He looked uncomfortable. 'I did not like the girl.'

Alicia's lips twitched. 'Did she fancy you, perhaps? She was very pretty.'

'She once offered herself to me, yes.' Francesco looked down his nose in distaste. 'I refused.'

'Before I arrived in Montedaluca?'

'Yes.'

'She was one of the people who was most hostile to me. I see why now.'

'I swear I did not encourage her!'

'You didn't have to. You're a very attractive man, Francesco.' She smiled. 'Otherwise I wouldn't have kept your photograph on my bedroom wall.'

His eyes lit with pleasure. 'I had forgotten that. Do you still have it?'

She hadn't the heart to lie. 'Yes. It's stored in a box with all my rugby pin-ups.'

'So I am one of a crowd.' He shrugged. 'That is better than torn to pieces and thrown away.'

'Let's get back to Cinzia,' said Alicia. 'You think the instructions were from her?'

'I do. *Indubbiamente*. Also that disgusting garment. I got rid of it before I left the hotel.' Francesco looked at her steadily. 'You were everything I wanted in a bride just as you were, Alicia. You had no need to—to embellish—is this the word?'

'"Bedizen" is more like it!' She shook her head. 'But at the time I was in too much of a state to even wonder why your mother gave me such a thing. Maybe Cinzia bought it to make me look ugly for you.'

'We shall never know. She left Montedaluca when my mother sent her away from the *castello*. I have not given her a thought since. Perhaps Giacomo might know.'

'It doesn't matter, Francesco. It's too late to bother about her now.'

'It is best for her that I do not find her,' he said grimly.

'We don't know that she was to blame.'

'She had to be,' he said with conviction. 'I cannot believe that my mother was guilty of such a thing.'

'I admit, I find it hard myself.' Alicia looked at her watch. 'What time should we be setting off? I need a shower and time to wrestle with my hair.'

'Is an hour long enough for you?'

'Of course. By the way, where did the pastries come from?'

'I went out to buy them while you were sleeping.' Francesco smiled smugly as he collected the tray. 'But I made the coffee with my own hands.'

The journey to Montedaluca took less than an hour, but Alicia wished it could have been twice as long when the ancient town walls came into view. In spite of Francesco's promise that things would be different, the butterflies in Alicia's stomach were on the rampage as they drove past the car parks used by visitors and entered through the old Roman arch. There were smiles and waves as Francesco's car was recognised. Alicia's tension mounted as they passed the main square with its central fountain, and the small, elegant hotel where she had stayed with her mother and the Davies family the night before the wedding. The narrow streets leading from it had shops that kept the inhabitants supplied with food, and others that stocked expensive gifts for the tourists that thronged the town at this time of year. Alicia's fingernails bit into her palms when they reached the cathedral, but her spirits sank even further as they left the town to take the steep, winding road to the *castello*.

Francesco drove very slowly up the winding, cypress-lined approach to the castle. Above the dark, pointing fingers of the trees the ancient towers loomed against the brilliant blue sky, looking even more forbidding to Alicia now than the first time she'd seen them. Francesco parked at the foot of the worn, marble stone steps leading up to the massive door, and Giacomo immediately appeared and hurried to greet them.

'*Benvenuto contessa.*' The neat, ageless man smiled warmly at Alicia as Francesco took her hand to help her from the car.

'*Grazie. Com'esta*, Giacomo?' she returned after a split second of surprise.

He assured her he was well, and seized the bags Francesco had taken from the car. He confirmed that all was also well within the *castello*, and the ladies were waiting on the terrace where lunch would be served in thirty minutes, if that was convenient for *la contessa*.

'Is it, Alicia?' asked Francesco, the gleam in his eye betraying that he knew she was taken aback, both by the welcome and the use of her title. 'Tell the ladies that we will go up to our room with the luggage and will be with them shortly,' he told Giacomo, and, still keeping her hand firmly in his grasp, led Alicia across the lofty hall.

Nothing had changed. The walls—which instead of the stern, unembellished stone she'd pictured before her first visit—were still painted the same soft ochre-red, with great sconces at intervals big enough to accommodate dozens of candles. Twin staircases branched up to a gallery with a formal drawing room and dining room leading off it, and at either end the towers which housed the bedrooms. Which one, Alicia wondered, had been allotted to her? Instead of taking her luggage to the guest room she'd occupied before the wedding, Giacomo turned in the opposite direction to the suite of rooms she'd used just once, so exhausted by the demands of her long wedding day that she'd slept without even knowing that she'd shared a bed with her bridegroom.

'*Grazie*, Giacomo,' said Francesco in dismissal as the old man put the cases down. 'We shall be down in a few minutes.'

Alicia took in a deep breath as she looked at the intricately carved furniture, and the big tester-bed that dominated the room.

'If,' began Francesco, before she could say a word, 'we are to preserve the fiction of reconciliation—even a short time—we must share my rooms, Alicia, to convince the servants. Do not be alarmed. I shall sleep in my dressing room, but this is good because I shall be at hand if you have the nightmare again.'

Alicia nodded reluctantly. 'I suppose you're right. Now, if you'll excuse me I need time in the bathroom to make myself presentable enough to join the ladies. Incidentally, I was surprised by my welcome. Giacomo seemed genuinely pleased to see me.'

Francesco smiled crookedly. 'He is, *cara*. He worries that I am lonely.'

'And are you?'

He shrugged. 'Sometimes, yes. I work hard during the day, and in the evenings I dine alone, or with Zia Luisa and Bianca when Zia is well enough, and then fall weary into my bed. Most of my friends are married with families, and sometimes I am invited to dine with them, or I entertain them here. But Roberto Alva, an old friend who is now our local doctor, and still *solo*, sometimes asks me down to his place for a game of chess.' The brilliant eyes took on a sardonic gleam. 'It must sound most dull compared with your life, Alicia.'

'What about all these ladies you discourage by telling them about me?' she demanded.

He shrugged. 'I do not seek such pleasures in Montedaluca, or even in Florence, where I am also known. If the need for feminine company becomes pressing, I go to Rome and look up old acquaintances.'

Alicia's eyebrows rose. 'And are these acquaintances always ready to drop everything to—to accommodate your *pressing* need?'

Again the shrug. 'Since the ladies in question are widows or divorcees, or successful businesswomen who have chosen to stay single, they usually find time to dine with me.'

I bet they do, thought Alicia acidly. She looked down at her linen trousers and tailored cotton shirt. 'If I put my jacket on will I do, Francesco?'

He nodded slowly as his eyes moved over her in leisurely appreciation. 'Yes,' he said simply. 'You will do very well indeed. You have much style now, Alicia.'

'Thank you. But it's all down to Bron that I go to work looking smart. I wear jeans and T-shirts otherwise.'

'Then wear them here, also.' He smiled. 'You looked delightful in those jeans yesterday. As you did the first time I saw you.'

She smiled wryly. 'I've moved on a bit since then, Francesco.'

A few minutes later, make-up touched up and every curl imprisoned in the severe knot she'd kept to for her return to the *castello*, Alicia slid her arms into the jacket he held for her and squared her shoulders. 'Right. Shall we go?'

'First I must ask you to wear this, Alicia.' Francesco held out his hand, and she tensed as she saw the wide gold ring in his palm.

'So that's why you held my hand—you were concealing my bare ring-finger from Giacomo.'

'It also gave me much pleasure to hold this little hand in mine.' Francesco slid the ring on the third finger, startled her by raising the hand to his lips, then opened the door. 'Come then, *contessa*.'

She winced. 'Please don't call me that.'

'If we are to convince others that we are reunited, it is best you get accustomed to it.' He took her hand again to lead her out onto the gallery, and through the formal dining room with its big, carved fireplace and tall glass doors, out onto a vast terrace she remembered only too vividly. Its stone columns, softened by entwining greenery, had made a superb setting for their wedding feast. It had also been the scene of her first meeting with Francesco's mother. Alicia batted the thought away as she looked out over the panoramic view of vine-covered Tuscan hills and silvery olive groves.

But this time there was no cold, elegant woman giving out rays of disapproval to mar Alicia's pleasure. Instead the two ladies sitting at the table at one end of the terrace beamed as they approached, and the younger sprang up, hands outstretched.

'*Contessa*, how lovely to see you! And you too, of course, Signor Francesco,' she added with a smile.

'*Grazie*, Bianca,' he said dryly.

Alicia grasped the hands, smiling warmly. 'How do you do, Bianca?' She moved to greet the older woman, smiling down into the lined, handsome face that lit with pleasure as Alicia bent to kiss both soft, powdered cheeks. '*Signora*, how are you?'

'I am well, Alicia, but why "*signora*"?' retorted the old lady. 'Am I not Zia Luisa now you are the grown up lady?'

Alicia laughed. 'I was just waiting for permission, Zia Luisa.'

'Ring the bell, *carina*, so Giacomo knows we're ready,' said Francesco, holding a chair for her.

It was strange to ring the bell that no one but Francesco's mother had ever dared touch, and even more so to sit in her chair. It brought it home to Alicia that *she* was now the *contessa*, and must behave accordingly if the charade was to be successful. She smiled at Francesco as he sat beside her. 'I'd forgotten the wonderful view from here.'

'Or perhaps you would not let yourself remember it?' he said in an undertone.

'Perhaps.'

Giacomo arrived with a tray of assorted *crostini*, and then presented a bottle of wine to Francesco for approval before filling the glasses.

'*Grazie*, Giacomo,' said Alicia, and with a bow the smiling man left them to their meal.

'Now,' said Zia Luisa as she selected a morsel of crisp, toasted bread spread with pâté, 'Francesco says you had an interesting job, Alicia. Tell us all about it. But talk slowly. I have not spoken much English since you were last here, *cara*.'

Had a job? Was she supposed to have given it up, or was Zia Luisa just rusty on her tenses? Alicia shot a questioning look at Francesco. 'Yes,' she agreed smoothly. 'It's interesting work. I've been very busy lately.'

'It is to do with the rugby football?' said Bianca.

Alicia agreed that it was, and tried to give the ladies an idea of what her work entailed. They listened, enthralled, amazed at a career in such a masculine environment.

'My wife has been very successful,' said Francesco. 'But she has also worked very hard. She needs rest.'

'You must sleep a lot, as I do, *cara*,' said his great-aunt, with a twinkle in her blue da Luca eyes. 'Keep her in bed in the mornings, Francesco.'

'I will do my best, Zia,' he promised, poker faced, and refilled the old lady's wine glass.

Alicia refused more wine. She needed a clear head. Because one thing was becoming clearer by the minute. Their smiling encouragement made it plain that Zia Luisa and Bianca believed the reconciliation was for real.

'We ordered just a light lunch for today,' said Bianca, when cheese and fruit were served to finish the meal. 'But Pina has something more substantial planned for dinner, and is waiting for your instructions, *contessa*, as to your wishes for other meals.'

'My first wish,' said Alicia promptly, 'is that you call me by my name, Bianca, not the title.'

'I should be most happy,' said the woman, delighted, and turned to Zia Luisa, who was nodding in her chair. 'And now I must help the *signora* to bed for her nap. She does very well for her age, but she tires easily.' Bianca smiled fondly. 'And she so enjoys her two glasses of wine.'

'Unlike Alicia, who has barely touched one,' commented Francesco, and got up to assist his aunt to her feet. He spoke to her gently in her own tongue, and she touched a hand to his face, smiled drowsily at Alicia, and let Bianca lead her away to the bedrooms in the other tower.

'So,' said Francesco, resuming his seat. 'You have survived lunch with the ladies of the house, Alicia, but you have eaten very little.'

'I was a bit tense,' she admitted. 'Not least because both Bianca and Zia Luisa seem to think I'm back here for good.'

He shrugged. 'When they knew you were coming to stay, they were so pleased I had persuaded you to return to me I could not disillusion them. And now you are here it is only sensible to let them think—as we need others to think,' he added significantly, 'That we are reconciled.'

CHAPTER EIGHT

ALICIA sat very still, looking at but not seeing the view while Francesco peeled a peach. He sliced it, put it on her plate and touched her hand.

'Eat, Alicia.'

She came to with a start and looked down at the luscious fruit. 'Oh. Thank you.' She smiled as she tasted a sliver. 'Mmm, delicious.'

'You always liked the peaches here.'

She raised an eyebrow as she looked up. 'My "always" here was so brief I'm surprised you remember that.'

He brushed back a lock of hair the breeze had ruffled. 'I remember everything about you, Alicia. I was very much in love with my little English *fidanzata*.'

'Welsh,' she corrected, to hide the sudden, unwanted wave of emotion that swept over her. 'Or British, if you prefer.'

He smiled slowly. 'You do not like me to speak of how I felt?'

She ate another slice of peach. 'We are not the same people we were then, Francesco. After years of trying to hate you—'

'Trying?' His eyes lit with heat that set her pulse leaping as he leaned nearer.

Her chin lifted. 'It was impossible to change from one emotion to the other with a flick of a switch, like a machine. Even if you didn't want me I couldn't stop loving you—though I had a darned good try!'

'And in time you succeeded?'

'I thought I had. Completely. But since I'm now here in Montedaluca, in the last place on earth I ever thought I'd come back to again, I suppose I didn't have quite as much success as I thought.' She turned in relief as Giacomo appeared with a coffee tray. *'Grazie.'* She smiled at him, glad of the interruption as he removed the used plates. With an effort of will she mustered all the Italian she could remember to tell him that she would go down to see Pina later.

'Now you've spoken to him in his own tongue—with that delightful accent—Giacomo is your slave forever,' remarked Francesco, after the smiling man had left them.

'I won't be here that long.'

'You told me you have two weeks of holiday. You must at least stay for that—if you wish to convince Gareth we are reconciled,' he added with emphasis.

Alicia was pretty sure it would take a lot longer than two weeks to do that, but didn't say so in case Francesco took it as encouragement. Did he really want her to stay as long as possible? She gazed in thoughtful silence at the idyllic panorama before her. Now she was here, it would be no hardship. Not least because the *castello* felt so much more welcoming without the glacial presence of Francesco's mother.

'Is it so difficult for you to remain here for a while?' he demanded.

'If you want the truth—'

'I probably do not. But say it anyway.'

'It's not as difficult as I thought it would be, because there's a more relaxed atmosphere.'

'Now my mother is no longer here,' he said, resigned.

'Yes. I tried so hard to please her, to make her like me, but of course it's not possible to *make* someone like you.' Alicia came to a decision. 'But, now we're talking about this in a reasonable way, you should know exactly why I ran away in Paris.'

Francesco frowned, surprised, and moved his chair nearer. 'I thought I knew well why you ran. I said such terrible things, I broke your heart.'

'It wasn't just the things you said that did that. Probably you'd have won me round in a little while because I was so much in love with you.' Alicia took in a deep breath. 'What tipped the scale was the bitter hurt of what the *contessa* had done. I was so thrilled to get her present, but, when I saw your appalled reaction to my attempt to please you as she instructed, I couldn't believe she'd been so cruel. Of course, I realise now that it must have been Cinzia's doing. But I didn't know that at the time. I had ignored my misgivings before the wedding because I loved you so desperately, and believed you loved me. But your disgust, combined with the *contessa*'s apparent cruelty, made the prospect of my future at Montedaluca unbearable.'

Francesco said something under his breath and refilled her coffee cup. 'Drink it, Alicia. Your face is white again.'

'I have pale skin, remember?' She smiled crookedly. 'It goes with the hair.'

'One thing you must believe,' he said urgently. 'I did love you. I adored you. Can you imagine my feelings when I heard you were seen getting into a car that evening, Alicia?' His handsome face darkened. 'I pictured such terrible things—kidnap, or worse.'

She bit her lip. 'But I rang you, Francesco.'

'That cold little message was supposed to comfort me?'

'I didn't want to comfort you!' She cleared her throat impatiently as her voice cracked.

'Tell me what happened,' he said quietly.

Alicia took a deep, calming breath. 'I shot out of the hotel to hail a taxi, hoping to catch the Eurostar, but there was no cab in sight. An elderly couple were loading their car outside. They saw me crying, and offered me a lift home via the ferry.'

'You told them you were running away from your husband?' he demanded.

She flashed him a scornful look. 'Of course not. I said I'd quarrelled with my boyfriend and was desperate to get home to my mother. They were really lovely people, showed me their passports as identity, even gave me their son's telephone number to ring in case I needed confirmation. But all I needed was to get away from you. So my kind Samaritans took me back to the UK, and eventually even put me on a train to Cardiff. You know the rest.'

Francesco was silent for a long time, his face set in sombre lines. When he spoke his voice was harsh. 'It is no wonder you hate me.'

'I don't any more, Francesco.' She managed a smile. 'As I've said more than once, it's time to forget the past and go on from here.'

He turned to look at her. 'Go on?'

'Well, yes. We can't go back.'

'If you were not so worried about Gareth, would you have agreed to stay here for a while?'

'Probably not. I only came to sign some papers, remember. But in the circumstances it's a practical idea.' Alicia shrugged. 'I've only just split up with Jason, so if he heard I'd acquired some other man in my life right away Gareth wouldn't believe it. But to avoid hurting his parents and Megan—which is the whole point of all this where Bron and I are concerned—he must hear we're together again, Francesco. And once he does he won't be able do a thing about it—except try to rearrange your pretty face,' she added flippantly.

His face hardened. 'I repeat, Alicia, he would not find that so very easy.'

'That's what my mother said.'

'*Cosa?*'

'You were the first one Bron thought of as a deterrent for Gareth. And because you were a rugby player too, she was sure you'd be able to take care of yourself.'

His eyebrows rose. 'I am most gratified. When I see her, I will thank her.'

Alicia tried to stifle a yawn. 'Sorry! All this emotion is exhausting stuff. Would you mind if I follow Zia Luisa's example and have a rest?'

'No, *carina*.' Francesco got up quickly. 'It is a very good idea. You slept very little last night.'

'I've been sleeping very little any night for a while, due to Bron's revelations on top of the fright Gareth gave me.'

On the way back to their tower, Alicia looked round at the grandeur of the dining room she'd found so overwhelming when she'd eaten there every night with Francesco and the *contessa* at a table big enough for a banquet. 'Does Zia Luisa get up for dinner these days?'

'Sometimes, sometimes not. But we no longer eat in here unless we have guests. When I reduced the staff, I ordered dinner to be served in the small room which opens on the *loggia* downstairs, sometimes on the *loggia* itself on warm evenings. It is easier for Pina, and much—what is the word?'

'Cosier?'

He smiled. '*Esattamente*. I cannot imagine living anywhere else but here at the *castello*, but I do not require the formality that my mother demanded.'

'Understandable, when she'd never known anything different.'

Francesco shook his head as he opened the door to their suite. 'That is not true, though it is the impression she strived to give. When she met my father she was working in her father's hotel in Milano. She was very beautiful as a girl.'

'She was still beautiful when I met her,' said Alicia. 'So your father fell in love with her?'

'Possibly. Mamma confided very little. It was Zia Luisa who told me my father had enjoyed the company of many women in his life, but had managed to avoid marrying any of them. Then at the age of fifty-six he suddenly acquired a bride.' Francesco smiled wryly. 'Fortunately, since I was born just nine months after the wedding, my resemblance to my father is unmistakeable.'

'I know, I've seen the photographs.' Alicia stacked the pillows against the carved headboard of the bed and curled up against them, her eyes thoughtful. 'No wonder your mother was disappointed with your choice of *fidanzata*. She'd obviously set her heart on a truly aristocratic bride for you, not a little nobody with a dodgy pedigree like me. How about her family? I don't remember meeting any of them at the wedding.'

'She refused to invite them. When she was young her father owned a small *trattoria*, but in time he expanded and began buying other properties. Instead of waiting on tables in the *trattoria*, Sophia began work as receptionist in the new hotel in Milano, and so met my father. To marry Conte Ettore da Luca was a great triumph for her. Papa Lusardi provided his daughter with a very acceptable dowry, which included the apartment building in Florence, but he himself was not socially acceptable to her after her grand marriage so they became estranged. I went to visit him with news of her death, and invited him to stay here for her funeral, and it was touching to see him grieve for his daughter. I never knew until Mamma was ill that her cold dignity was a mask to conceal her humble origins.' Francesco sat down on the chaise between the windows, his legs outstretched. 'My father died when I was a small child. I hardly remember him. Whatever her faults, my mother was the rock in my life, Alicia. I loved her very much.'

'I know. And I'm glad you told me about her. It explains a lot.' Alicia's eyes narrowed. 'It proves that Cinzia was most definitely the culprit. Your mother, whatever her origins, had faultless taste. I should have realised that she couldn't have given me such a tacky nightgown, even less the instructions that went with it.'

'*Daverro.*' Francesco got up. 'I will leave you to rest, Alicia. When you are ready, come back to the *terrazzo* and I will send for tea. Or would you like it now?'

'No thanks.' She sighed. 'Actually, I'd better get up, Francesco. I promised to have a word with Pina.'

'No, sleep for a while. I shall take you to see Pina later.' He crossed to the bed and gave her the smile that still had the power to turn her heart over. 'I am so very glad you agreed to come, Alicia.'

She dropped her eyes to hide her response. 'You left me no choice, really. When do we go to see the—what did you call him?—the *notaio*?'

'We do not go to him. Signor Raimondi will come here tomorrow at eleven.'

'Francesco.'

He paused on his way to the door, eyebrows raised.

Alicia smiled wryly. 'I thought I'd only be here a day or two, so I didn't bring many clothes, and dinner was very formal in your mother's day. Is the dress I wore last night suitable?'

'It is a beautiful dress, but keep it for another occasion, *cara*. Wear jeans tonight if you wish.'

She shook her head. 'Not for dinner with Zia Luisa.'

'Your clothes were unpacked while we had lunch, Alicia, so all will be ready for you. But not the dress. I have plans for that,' he informed her.

Alicia eyed the closed door, wondering what plans he had in mind, then slid off the bed and crossed to the wardrobe to find everything she owned hanging there, freshly ironed and immaculate.

Alicia returned to her pillows and lay looking at the view from the tall windows. So, she'd not only survived her return to Montedaluca, it had been less of an ordeal than expected. No ordeal at all, really. From the moment she'd seen Giacomo smiling at her in welcome her tension had begun to fade. And her warm reception by Zia Luisa and Bianca Giusti had banished it completely.

In no mood to sleep, Alicia took out her phone and rang her mother again. 'I'm here at the *castello*, Bron,' she announced, then went on to explain about the stop in Florence, and why she'd only just arrived in Montedaluca. 'The thing is,' she said carefully, 'I'm staying on here for a while. Just as you suggested, I'm enlisting my husband as protection against Gareth.'

'Are you, indeed?' said Bron, surprised. 'Was Francesco happy to agree to that?'

'It was his idea.' Alicia told her about the nightmare. 'Apparently I was screaming at Gareth in my sleep, so I just had to tell Francesco about our problem. He promptly suggested that the best way to solve it was to convince Gareth that my husband and I are no longer *separato*, as he put it.'

'Promptly?' said Bron. 'No sacrifice, then?'

'There's a snag.'

'Isn't there always?'

'His great-aunt Zia Luisa, and Bianca Giusti, the lady who taught me Italian—she now lives here, as a sort of companion for Zia—both took it for granted we're back together when they heard I was coming to stay.'

'Are you having problems with that?'

'Only a constant feeling of unreality. One minute I was dashing about in a world centred on rugby players and press interviews and the Six Nations, and the next I'm back here in the last place I ever intended to set foot in again. With just one ex-rugby player. But here's the weird bit,' she added. 'I am now the *contessa*.'

Bron chuckled. 'How very grand! By the way, have you been to the solicitor to see about your legacy yet?'

'No. Tell George we're so posh here the solicitor comes to us. I'll keep you posted.'

'Hold on, darling,' said Bron urgently. 'You need to get the news to Gareth pretty sharply. So ring Megan. She'll do the rest.'

'Oh what tangled webs, and all that,' sighed Alicia. 'But you're right, Bron. As usual. Love to George.'

When Francesco came back Alicia was standing by the window, ready, if not hugely willing, to confront Pina, the diva who ruled over the kitchen.

'Did you sleep?' he asked.

'No. I had a chat with Bron instead. What have you been doing?'

'Inspecting the gardens with Antonio.' Francesco ran a hand through his hair. 'You look so perfect I must take a few minutes in the bathroom to make myself worthy of you. Then we shall go down to Pina.'

Just as though they'd been married for years. Which, of course, they had been, if one counted from the day of their wedding until now. Alicia's mouth turned down. To actually feel married you needed a normal marriage. And there was nothing normal about hers, though the unreality part was fading worryingly fast. And if their little comedy helped solve the problem with Gareth she would act it out to Oscar-winning standard for as long as it took. Which was utterly pointless, of course, unless Gareth heard about it. So this evening she would ring Megan with the news, which would then go straight to Gareth via the usual Davies grapevine. Meg would be furious with her when she eventually found out it was all a charade, but that couldn't be helped.

The visit to Pina went off surprisingly well with Francesco as interpreter. Alicia soon found that the Italian vocabulary she'd done her best to forget was filtering back now she was hearing it spoken around her, and with lots of smiling and arm waving, and the occasional help from Francesco, she managed to communicate with the cook, who was generously curved and flashing of eye. Pina introduced Teresa, the young girl who helped in the kitchen or the house as required, then informed the *contessa* that for dinner that evening she had prepared *involtini divitelo*, which Francesco translated as veal rolled in ham and sage leaves.

'*Delizioso,*' said Alicia, smiling, and thanked Pina warmly when the woman suggested that the *contessa* might enjoy tea on the *loggia*.

Alicia left the big kitchen with Francesco, feeling much reassured. During her previous stay she'd had little contact with Pina.

'So. It is not as bad as you thought?' said Francesco.

'No.' Alicia smiled wryly as they made for the *loggia*. 'No one so far seems to find it the least strange that I'm back here at the *castello*.'

Francesco's face assumed a look of chilling hauteur. 'Even if they did, no one would be unwise enough to say so.'

Alicia sat in the chair he pulled out for her at a round table with a *pietra dura* top. 'You can be horribly forbidding at times, Francesco.'

He shrugged and took a chair opposite her, frowning into the late-afternoon sunshine. 'Have no fear, Alicia. My wife will be treated with the utmost respect.'

'Even though she ran away from you?'

'You came back,' he said flatly.

'But Francesco, I haven't really—' She stopped as Teresa arrived with a laden tray and set it down carefully in front of her.

'*Grazie*, Teresa,' said Alicia, and the girl smiled shyly and hurried away.

'Zia Luisa stays in her room until dinner time, which gives Bianca time to herself at this time of day, so the tea is all yours,' said Francesco.

'And the coffee, no doubt, is for you,' said Alicia, noting the two pots. 'Shall I pour for you?'

'*Grazie*.' He leaned his elbows on the table to watch her, his smile so sardonic she eyed him narrowly. 'You were going to say that you are not really back, Alicia. But you must pretend that you are. And pretend well. Otherwise how will we convince anyone—most importantly Gareth—that we are no longer *separato*?'

Alicia poured herself a cup of tea. The real thing, she noted; no teabags here. 'I know, Francesco. I'll try.'

He leaned nearer. 'I do not even have to try. To me it seems the most natural thing in the world to sit here with you again.'

'Again? You never sat here with me last time,' she retorted. 'I took afternoon tea with your mother on the *terrazzo* upstairs, while she instructed me on the proper behaviour for a Contessa da Luca.'

Francesco frowned. 'Then did you not think it extraordinary to receive such a gift from her?'

'Of course I did. It was a huge shock. I was educated by nuns, remember? But for all I knew it was the custom here for brides to deck themselves out like that, and you'd expect me to look that way.' She shook her head in disgust. 'I can't believe I was so stupid!'

Francesco shook his head. 'Innocent, not stupid, Alicia.'

'Ignorant, you mean.'

'Sometimes my English is not perfect, remember.'

'Never mind.' She gave him a mocking smile. 'With looks like yours, it doesn't matter.'

To her surprise he looked embarrassed. 'Looks are an accident of nature, Alicia.' His eyes gleamed. 'But, if they first attracted you to me, I am grateful for them.'

Alicia's eyes fell from the intent blue gaze. 'They were certainly your entry into my rugby hall of fame. You were by far the best looking man on my wall. Which is not such a huge compliment,' she added wryly.

'I know it. Rugby players are chosen for skill and strength, not looks. For me it was not my face but my speed which won me a place in the team.' He reached a hand across the table to touch hers. 'But I give thanks for this face if it brought us together, Alicia. I shall never forget your look of wonder that first day in Florence.'

She smiled crookedly. 'I thought I was dreaming.'

'As did I when I first saw *your* face.' His grasp tightened. 'I took one look and lost my heart.'

Alicia snatched her hand away so he couldn't feel her pulse racing. 'Why do you keep bringing up the past, Francesco? That was then, and this is now.'

'And now,' he said, suddenly implacable, 'We are here together again. As far as the world is concerned, we are reconciled.'

'But we know we're not. It's just convenient fiction,' she said flatly.

Francesco rose to his feet, a very unsettling look in his eyes. 'If we pretend long enough, *cara*, who knows? Perhaps it will become fact.'

'I seriously doubt that,' she retorted, wishing she could run up to the bedroom and hide until dinner. But since it was the master bedroom, and Francesco was the master, fat chance of that.

He held out his hand. 'Let us walk in the gardens to admire Antonio's work for a while. It may give you an appetite for dinner.'

'All right. I'll come for the walk,' she said reluctantly.

'But you will not take my hand?'

'I'm wearing the ring now, so it isn't necessary.'

His mouth tightened. 'Is my touch so—so repugnant?'

'No, it's not. I just need time to get used to you again,

Francesco.' Not for the world would she admit that his touch still had the power to make her pulse race.

'*Va bene.* Let us walk, then.'

The gardens of the *castello* descended in tiers, with flowers and shrubs giving way to evergreens and cypresses as the terrain grew steeper, and at intervals water gushed from the mouths of gargoyles in the ancient walls and ran off into subterranean cisterns equipped with pumps that recycled the water back again. Alicia felt the timeless peace of the place seeping through her as she looked out on the sunlit panorama of vines and olive groves and meandering roads lined with tall, pointing cypress. When they reached the grassy terrace that marked a halfway point on the descent, Francesco gestured at a carved wooden seat beneath a pergola wreathed with greenery.

'The sun is less fierce now. Would you like to sit here for a while?'

Alicia nodded and sat down. 'It's so lovely here. Surely Antonio doesn't manage all this on his own?'

'He has help.' Francesco sat beside her, pointedly keeping his distance. 'Two men from the town, both retired now, come three days a week.'

They sat in surprisingly companionable silence for a while, then Francesco turned to look at her. 'Alicia, last night, when you had the nightmare, you did not object to my touch.'

'No,' she said soberly. 'I was very grateful for it. You were a tremendous comfort. I haven't had nightmares for ages, not since—'

'You ran away from me?'

She nodded.

'I take the blame for your early nightmares, but Gareth is responsible for new ones.' His eyes hardened. 'He frightened you very badly, no?'

'It wasn't fright, exactly. It just felt so horribly wrong. Gareth has kissed my cheek and hugged me often enough in the past, and I've never given it a thought. But that night it was different.'

'Because he wanted to be your lover.'

'Yes.' She shivered.

'Therefore,' Francesco said with decision, 'We must play our parts well to convince him this will never happen. For me this is easy. For you, obviously, it is not.'

Alicia felt sudden compunction. Francesco was trying to help her out, for heaven's sake, and she was an ungrateful idiot. She knew, of old, that he was a tactile man.

She turned to him in sudden curiosity. 'Francesco—when I came to stay those weeks before the wedding why were you so distant with me?'

His mouth turned down. 'I was afraid to touch you.'

'But why?'

'It was torture to have you near and yet not near enough, Alicia. I plunged myself into work as much as possible to stay away from you.' He turned his head to meet her eyes. 'I wanted you so much it was driving me mad. Surely you knew that?'

'No. I had no idea.' She gazed at him, astonished. 'I was afraid you'd changed your mind.'

He let out a snort of derision. 'I had not, believe me, *cara*. My mother knew well how I felt. She warned me that I must not give way to the base desires that drive all men. She told me that if I insisted on an innocent, untried girl for a bride, you must remain so until after the ceremony.' He threw out a hand in a dismissive gesture. 'It was relief when your mother arrived and took you to stay with her at the hotel.'

Alicia shook her head in wonder. 'And I thought you were avoiding me.'

'I was,' he said simply, and looked at his watch. '*Allora*, we should go back. Zia Luisa dines downstairs tonight because you are here, therefore we shall eat early.'

Feeling it was time for an olive branch, Alicia took his hand to walk up the steep path through the gardens.

'*Grazie*,' he said softly, his fingers closing on hers.

'*Prego*.'

And as simply as that peace was declared. Even the matter of who got ready first was settled just as amicably when they reached their rooms.

'I have a request,' Francesco said as he closed the door behind them.

'What is it?'

'Will you wear your hair loose tonight?' His eyes gleamed like jewels in the fading light as he touched a hand to her severe knot.

She smiled demurely. 'Yes, Francesco.'

He grinned. 'I like so much to hear you say that. Say it more often, *per favore*.'

'Yes, Francesco,' she said obediently, laughing at him, and felt her heart melt at the obvious pleasure he took in the sound.

'I like so much to hear you laugh also, Alicia!'

'But now I have a request,' she said firmly. 'I need the bathroom first so I can use my hairdryer while you're in the shower. This isn't easy hair, Francesco.'

'But very beautiful. *Va bene*, I shall wait until you call.' He strolled, whistling, to the dressing room, unaware that he'd brought a lump to her throat. Taking his hand had been such a simple thing to do, yet it had obviously made him happy. Her eyes widened. It had made her happy too.

Alicia was finally ready in the newly ironed silk shirt, and a slim, cream linen skirt worn in deference to Zia Luisa. Francesco's eyes were warm with approval as they moved over the shining hair she'd left loose.

'*Grazie*. You look beautiful, *cara*.'

So did he, in perfectly tailored pale linen trousers, a jacket a shade or two darker, and wonderful shoes, as always.

'You look good too,' she assured him.

'But before we go down,' said Francesco quietly, 'I have something I hope you will wear.'

Alicia's heart gave a thump as she saw he was holding a small, velvet box. 'The betrothal ring,' she said, resigned.

He shook his head. 'I know you did not like it. You have agreed to wear the wedding ring because it is necessary, I know.

But this is a ring I had made to give to you on our wedding night, after—' His jaw clenched.

'After we'd made love for the first time?' she said quietly.

He nodded, and opened the box to display a cluster of diamonds set like a delicate posy on a plain gold band, as unlike the heavy ruby betrothal ring as it was possible for a ring to be. 'Will you wear it, Alicia?'

She nodded silently, and held out her hand for him to slide the ring on her finger. 'It's exquisite,' she said huskily, and gave him a shaky smile. 'How did you know it would fit?'

'It is the size of your wedding ring,' he said simply, and held out his hand. 'Come. Let us go.'

'Could you go on down, Francesco? I need to ring Megan.'

He nodded quickly. '*Va bene*. Make sure you convince her, Alicia. I will come back for you in ten minutes.'

Meg was astounded when Alicia gave her the news. 'You're really getting back together?'

'Yes,' said Alicia, glad Meg couldn't see her face. 'Things began to change for me the moment I heard Francesco had gone to Cardiff straight away to look for me.' That, at least, was the gospel truth. 'And apparently he still has feelings for me.' That was true, too, though Alicia wasn't perfectly sure what the feelings were.

Meg, as usual, gave a string of instructions to Alicia about being careful, passed on a message to Francesco to take great care of her, then ended the phone call so she could ring Hay and give her parents the news, by which time Francesco had returned.

'What did Megan say?'

'She was astounded.' Alicia pulled a face. 'But she sent you her regards, and told you to take care of me.'

'I will take great pleasure in that,' he said gravely, and held out his hand.

This time Alicia took it without hesitation, glad of its warm clasp as they descended the sweep of the stairs to the hall below.

CHAPTER NINE

THE evening with Zia Luisa and Bianca was a success, not least because the small room where they ate dinner was so much more comfortable and intimate than the great *sala da pranzo*, and Alicia enjoyed Pina's meal far more than any dinner eaten at the castello in the past.

'After tonight, Alicia, you must order what *you* like to eat,' said the handsome old lady, her eyes twinkling. 'But tonight Pina has indulged me with my favourite *dolce*. Have you had *zuccotto* before, *cara*?'

'I don't think so. What is it?'

'A sponge cake filled with nuts, chocolate and cream,' said Bianca, eyes shining at the prospect.

Francesco smiled wryly. 'My mother refused to let Pina serve it.'

'Sophia said it was bad for many things, including the figure,' said Luisa, and beamed. 'But at my age who cares if I am fat? And you, Alicia, have no worry about such things.'

'She is perfect the way she is,' agreed Francesco, smiling at Alicia as the women nodded in enthusiastic agreement.

'How is your charming mother, Alicia?' asked Bianca.

Both women listened with pleasure to news of Bronwen's marriage, and also Megan's.

'Your young friend was such a pretty bridesmaid at your

wedding,' said Luisa. 'And Bronwen was much admired, Alicia. She looked much too young to be your mother.'

'She still does. My stepfather says we look like sisters.' Alicia looked up with a smile as Giacomo came in to put the *zuccotto* in front of her. '*Grazie*, Giacomo.' She asked him to tell Pina that the veal had been superb, then sliced the cake for him to serve.

When the meal was over Luisa declined coffee, and Bianca rose at once to accompany her upstairs.

'This has been a delightful evening, Alicia,' said the old lady. 'It is so good to have you back again. *Buona notte, cara.*'

When they were alone Francesco suggested they go outside to drink their coffee. 'It is a beautiful night. You would like this?'

'I certainly would.' She grinned at him as they went out onto the dimly lit *loggia*. 'I need time to recover from the *zuccotto*.'

He laughed. 'You liked it?'

'It was so delicious, only the risk of another nightmare kept me from devouring another plateful.' But Alicia shot him a troubled look as she filled the coffee cups.

'What is wrong?' asked Francesco. He took the chair next to her and pulled it close.

'I feel such a terrible fraud. Don't you think we should tell Zia and Bianca the truth?'

Francesco shook his head decisively. 'It is best we do not. Leave the truth until it is unavoidable, *carina*—by which time it may be different.'

Alicia was afraid to ask what he meant. Did he really want her to come back? And if he did, how would she feel about it? Going back was rarely successful, whatever the situation. Besides, she was a different person now from the schoolgirl who'd fantasised over the photograph of Francesco da Luca. She studied him, trying to be objective as her eyes moved over the aquiline da Luca profile, the heavy, waving hair, and the muscular grace of his relaxed body. Combined with the effortless charm that only occasionally revealed the steel behind it, Francesco da Luca was a very impressive package. And legally he was still her husband.

He turned towards her suddenly, startling her. 'Why do you look at me like that?'

'I was just thinking back to the day we met.' Not quite true, but it would do.

'Good thoughts?'

'Yes. You know, Francesco, I think you look even better now than you did then.'

His eyes widened. *'Grazie.'*

'Prego.'

Francesco smiled slowly. 'I can return the compliment, Alicia. You were irresistible in your innocence at eighteen. But now you are an experienced woman, you are so *seducente* you are even more irresistible.'

Not sure what *seducente* meant—though she had a good idea—Alicia thanked him politely. 'But I'm not sure I care for "experienced" as an adjective.'

He shrugged. 'Forgive me if it is not the right word—you know I have trouble with my English.'

'I know nothing of the kind!'

Francesco laughed. 'If only you were fluent in Italian I could express myself as I really wish.'

A prospect so fraught with risk Alicia firmly changed the subject. 'Megan and Rhys have bought a house,' she informed him.

'In Cardiff?'

She nodded. 'Rhys is working at the University Hospital there, and they've found a house in the same area.'

'You are still as close as ever to Megan?'

'Oh yes. The best friend I could ever have.' Alicia smiled wryly. 'She was worried that I'd be furious because she'd told you how to find me.'

'And were you?'

'I could never be furious with Meg.'

'Only with me.'

She met his eyes. 'I'm not any more.'

He smiled, with a power that set her heart racing. '*Bene*. I am glad.' He sobered, eyeing her closely. 'Are you tired, *carina*?'

'I am rather,' she admitted, and pulled a face. 'And tomorrow I have to face your solicitor.'

Francesco rose to his feet, holding out his hand. 'You will not face him alone. I shall be close by your side. Come.'

Alicia got up and meekly took the hand he offered. Just in case Giacomo or someone saw them as they went upstairs, she told herself. When they reached their rooms she found that a tray had been left by the bed, with glasses and two insulated jugs.

'I arranged for fruit juice and mineral water,' explained Francesco as he closed the door. 'If you wake in distress again you will need a drink.'

She turned to look at him. 'You're very thoughtful.'

He moved closer. 'If I make life here as comfortable and pleasant for you as possible, Alicia, perhaps you will stay longer.'

'I have only two weeks' holiday.'

'I know this,' he said darkly. 'You remind me so often. Sleep well, Alicia,' he added, and turned to the door.

'Where are you going?' she asked, surprised by a sudden, strong objection to being left alone.

'To my study, to work for a while,' he said curtly. '*Perche?*'

'I just wondered.'

'I will try not to disturb you when I return.'

'Must you work tonight?'

Francesco closed his eyes for an instant. 'Yes,' he said tightly. 'I must.' He strode out of the room, leaving her staring, offended, at the closed door.

Alicia stalked angrily into the bathroom to get ready for the night. Nothing had changed, then. It was just the same as all those years ago, when she'd pleaded with him to spend time with her instead of working so hard. She frowned at her reflection as the penny finally dropped. Last time he'd shut himself up with his work because he'd wanted to make love to her. And in those days they'd slept in different rooms—different parts of the *castello*, even. She let the breath out very slowly. Was that why he'd flung out of the room? When she'd agreed to come back to Montedaluca he'd known only too well that she'd refuse if there was any mention of sharing a bedroom. But there was a very logical reason for it now—to convince everyone at the *castello*, and Gareth at home, that she was truly reconciled with Francesco. The fact that Gareth didn't know this yet was irrelevant. He would soon hear the glad news via Meg. And in the meantime there was the night to get through, with Francesco sleeping only yards away in the adjoining room.

Wishing she'd brought a more conventional nightgown, Alicia got into camisole and briefs, wrapped herself in her dressing gown, and was halfway through her cleansing and toning drill when the great big flaw in their plan suddenly hit her smack between the eyes.

Down below, on the *loggia*, Francesco was morosely contemplating the same flaw. He had been aware of it all along. So far Alicia, hopefully, had not. If at the end of the two weeks she went home again and back to her job, it would be impossible to convince her family that she was truly reconciled with her husband. At the thought of massive Gareth Davies forcing himself on Alicia, Francesco saw red, and got up to pace like a restless panther. From the moment he'd first set eyes on her again he'd known he could never let her divorce him. One look had been enough to bring all the old feelings rushing back. Now, after only a day or two spent in her company, they were stronger than ever. His fists clenched. No man was going to take her from him again, least of all Gareth Davies.

But in a way, he reminded himself, he should be grateful to the man for frightening Alicia with his unwanted lust. Now she was back where she belonged at last, here at the *castello*. But not locked up against her will, as feared by the hot-headed Gareth. Francesco threw back his head to stare up at the stars. Now he must do everything in his power to persuade Alicia to stay. He wanted her here with him in the *castello*, in his bed and in his life, to make babies with her—not just da Luca heirs, as she had accused, but living tokens of their love.

Because, no matter how much she might try to deny it, he was sure that Alicia loved him still. Perhaps not in the trusting, innocent way as when she was young. He had changed that with a few brutal words that had cost him his bride. So, now he must convince her that he would never hurt her again. Which was not easy when he wanted her so much. He breathed in deeply, hoping fervently that she was asleep by now so he could shut himself in his dressing room away from temptation. At the mere thought of the word, desire for her rushed through him like a forest fire. How in God's name was he going to curb that desire without frightening her away again? Of course, he thought with sharp regret, she was no longer an innocent, untried teenager. There had been one lover he knew of, and probably more that he did not. But Alicia, understandably, was wary of close relationships. Therefore he must take great care not to frighten her away from the one he longed to hold her to for the rest of her life.

When Francesco very quietly opened his bedroom door his heart sank. The room was not in darkness and Alicia was not sleeping. She was sitting up in bed, reading, wearing something pink and clinging which left her shoulders bare. All that glorious hair was cascading loose, and the sprinkling of freckles shone, unconcealed, along her cheekbones.

'Hi,' said Alicia, smiling at him. 'Have you finished your work?'

Francesco gave up. A man could stand only so much. 'I had no work so demanding it had to be done tonight.' He moved to the end of the bed, looking down at her. 'I removed myself from temptation.'

So she'd been right. 'How noble of you, Francesco.'

'Yes,' he agreed morosely. 'I am amazed by such nobility.'

She smiled sweetly to hide her triumph. 'Is it a while since you've made any trips to Rome?'

He looked blank for a moment, then his eyes lit with a familiar blue gleam. 'It is some time since I sought feminine company in

Rome, yes. Even so, Alicia, I will not take advantage of our situation.' His eyes smouldered. 'But it is very hard for me to share a room and not want to make love to an alluring, desirable woman who, as you say in English, is my lawful wedded wife.'

The words wiped the smile off Alicia's face. 'Then I'll say goodnight and discuss the flaw in our plan in the morning.'

'I think I can survive a talk without falling on you with ravening lust,' he assured her suavely.

'Excellent.' She folded her arms across her chest. 'In that case, have you any suggestions about what happens when I go back home to resume my normal life? About convincing Gareth?'

'You must tell him that I have agreed to allow—'

'*Allow?*'

Francesco rolled his eyes. '*Mi dispiace,* I start again. You must convince him that we plan to see each other often while a replacement is found for you.'

She shook her head. 'Won't wash. That could happen very quickly.'

He sat on the edge of the bed, his eyes holding hers. 'So, tell him that you can never love him in the way he wants because you still love *me*.'

'Not what Gareth wants to hear!' Alicia tried to edge away from Francesco's warmth, but her body refused to cooperate.

His voice roughened. 'Promise that you will take care never to be alone with him, *tesoro*.'

Alicia's heart gave a thud. She could take all the *cara*s and *carina*s in her stride, but *tesoro* was the endearment Francesco had used only in private. 'What if he comes to see me again?'

'You have the *interfono* on your door. Do not let him in.'

'I can't just turn him away, Francesco! I'm very fond of him. He's the nearest thing to a brother I've ever had.'

'I know this, and I understand,' he told her, with such sympathy Alicia wanted to throw herself in his arms and cry her eyes out against his chest. 'But he must learn that he cannot have you in the way he desires.'

Nor can any other man, he thought grimly. Even if you will not admit it, Alicia da Luca, you are mine. He got up and stood looking down at her. 'I will spend a little time in the bathroom then leave you in peace to sleep.'

Alicia heaved a sigh. 'All right.' She gave him a wry little smile. 'This is all so strange, isn't it?'

'Not for me,' he said over his shoulder, and closed the bathroom door behind him.

Alicia lay back against the pillows, wishing Francesco had kept his distance instead of stirring up her senses with that unique scent of his, which had more to do with his pheromones than the Aqua di Parma he still used. It was a shock to find she wanted him now as much—more—as she ever had. *Hey, he's still the same man who trampled on your delicate young illusions,* she reminded herself. But the weak shot at sarcasm was no use. Why, oh why, did she have to be a one-man woman? She'd done her level best to fall in love with other men. Lord knew, she met enough of them in her job. But it was obvious, now, that the years of grief and resentment over Francesco had obscured the fact that she'd never stopped loving him. Once she'd been forced to admit that he wasn't quite the black-hearted villain she'd painted him, her heart made it clear that it still belonged to him. And always had.

The tell-tale heart leapt as Francesco emerged from the bathroom bare-chested, towelling his hair as he made for his dressing room. 'I regret to be so long. I needed a cold shower,' he said tersely. 'Goodnight, Alicia.'

'Goodnight,' she said forlornly, her eyes following him as he made for the door on the far side of the room. He left it open a crack, and she watched until his light went out then returned to her book. But after reading the same page several times without making sense of it she closed the book, turned out the lamp and with a sigh curled up in the big bed.

Alicia surfaced to darkness, sobbing, tears streaming down her face. But before she was even fully awake she was cradled against the haven of a warm, bare chest as Francesco soothed her with a stream of liquid Italian that comforted her even though she understood only half of it.

'Sorry I woke you,' she said thickly at last. 'I need a tissue. There's a box on the table.'

Francesco reached to switch on the lamp, and armed with a handful of tissues mopped her face gently. 'You had the nightmare again, *tesoro*?'

She shook her head. 'Not about Gareth. This was the old, bad dream I used to have.'

'About me?' His arms tightened as she nodded. 'What happens in this bad dream?'

'A replay of the scene in Paris.' Alicia blew her nose prosaically. 'I haven't had it for years.' She looked up at him in apology, her heart contracting when she saw that his eyes were wet.

'Your sobs hurt my heart,' he said, and kissed her hair. 'I will pour you a drink, *piccola*.'

'Thank you,' she whispered, willing the floodgates to stay shut.

Francesco slid off the bed and leaned over her to stack the pillows against the headboard. '*Allora*, you may sit up to drink some fruit juice, but then you must try to sleep.'

She heaved herself upright and wriggled until she was comfortable. 'At least you don't have to change the sheets tonight.'

'*Davverro*.' Francesco handed her the drink, eyeing her questioningly. 'If it is years since you dreamed this, why again tonight, Alicia?'

'Who knows?' she muttered, eyeing him over the rim of the glass. This time he hadn't bothered with a dressing gown, and wore white boxers, which confirmed that he still possessed the physique that had made him such a good rugby player. Broad shoulders and flat stomach tapered into slim hips and the muscular, long legs that had given him the necessary speed for a successful winger.

He shifted uncomfortably under her scrutiny. 'Why do you look at me like that?'

'I was just thinking what good shape you're in. What do you do for exercise these days?'

'I train at the local rugby club, which is a pet project of mine. I do some coaching there, and if the team has problems with injuries I even play in the odd game. I also ski when I can.' He took her empty glass. 'Now, sleep again.' He switched off the lamp, then walked to the windows and drew back the curtains to let moonlight flood the room. 'Is that better, Alicia?'

'Francesco.'

He turned, his profile outlined by the moonlight. 'Yes?'

She heaved in a deep, shaky breath. 'I don't want to be alone. Could you stay for a while?'

He stood utterly still for a moment, then walked very slowly to the bed to look down at her, his face a handsome, expressionless mask. 'You ask much.'

'Too much?'

'*Dio,*' he said in anguish, and pulled her up into his arms. 'Tell me to go. Now.'

She shook her head, and buried her hot face against his chest. 'Stay. Please.'

'If I do—'

'You'll make love to me?' she finished, her voice muffled, and felt his heart hammering against hers.

'*Daverro,*' he growled.

For answer she set her open mouth to his chest and touched the tip of her tongue to his hot skin. Francesco groaned and turned her face up, his eyes questioning for a moment, then blazing fiercely as he met the look in hers. Exerting every last shred of self-control, he bent his head slowly, giving her time to turn away. But when their lips met at last the kiss was so incendiary it set them both on fire. They collapsed on the bed together to lie full length in each other's arms, straining each other close as Francesco kissed her with a devouring hunger Alicia responded to so fiercely, his heart swelled with feelings he had kept at bay for so many years they threatened to overwhelm him.

'Alicia, *amore*,' he gasped, raising his head to look down at her. 'I want you so much I hurt.'

'I hurt too. Make me better,' she whispered, with a little smile he smothered with devouring kisses.

He slid the straps of her camisole down, his lips leaving her mouth to follow his caressing hands as he undressed her, telling her in two languages how beautiful she was and how much he desired her.

She gasped as his fingers and lips closed over the erect tips of firm, taut breasts, nothing like those of the teenage girl he had fallen in love with.

Francesco raised his head, his eyes alight with a desire which took away what breath Alicia had left.

'You are everything I have ever desired,' he assured her passionately. '*Ti amo*, Alicia. Is it possible that you can still love me?'

'I never dreamed it could be, but apparently it is,' she said shakily.

Sending up a prayer of thanks, Francesco set out to erase the memory of all other lovers in Alicia's past as he kissed and caressed her slender body. He wanted, needed, to inflame all her senses until she burned with the same hunger he was keeping at bay only by a supreme act of will. At last, when she was gasping and breathless, his skilled, seeking hand slid between her thighs, and she stiffened. He kissed her, going no further until she welcomed his caressing, invading tongue and gave him back all the heat and response he'd ever dreamed of. At last, when his skilled, questing caresses found the little hidden bud which sent sensation streaking through her, she reared up against him, pushing her hips against him in such wild demand that he felt like a god.

'*Francesco!*' she pleaded hoarsely, and he held her close for a moment, then caressed her parted thighs and positioned himself between them. His eyes locked with hers, he slowly pressed himself into the hot, tight sheath that closed round him in such exquisite sensation. He fought to stay still, every muscle rigid with the control he was exerting, while every instinct urged him to seek his body's release. He bent his head to kiss her, his tongue invading in substitute penetration, and she returned his kisses feverishly, her fingers digging into his shoulders.

'Now, now, now!' she urged, and Francesco's control snapped.

He surged inside her, then stopped dead at her smothered gasp as he breached a barrier so unexpected it sent his heart rocketing to his throat.

'*Amore!*' He gazed down at her in disbelief as her fingernails dug deeper.

'Don't stop,' she whispered.

'*Dio*, I cannot!' With a groan Francesco thrust home inside her until he was sheathed to the hilt. He stayed still, heart thudding, forbidding his body to move. 'I hurt you,' he said huskily against her mouth.

'Not—not much.'

'Why did you not tell me?' he demanded.

'How could I?'

Her hips made a sinuous little writhing movement which silenced him very effectively as Francesco began to make love to her with all the skill at his command, his senses taking over from his euphoric brain as with lips, hands and the thrusting strength of his body he gradually increased the tempo of their loving until he took her to the brink of fulfilment. He held her there at the very edge until he felt the first ripples of her orgasm caress him, and only then surrendered to the climactic bliss of his own release as she fell apart in his arms.

When he found the will to move again, Francesco turned on his side and pulled her close in a possessive embrace, one long leg thrown over her thighs.

Alicia lay motionless against his hard, hot body, hoping her heart would stop thumping soon and her lungs resume normal service. So it was done at last. But she had no regrets. It had to happen sometime. Her virginity—not without difficulty and an enormous amount of tiresome argument—had survived college and several years in a male-orientated workplace. Yet in the end, amazingly, she'd surrendered it to the man who should have received the gift in the first place.

'Francesco,' she said at last, when it seemed unlikely he was going to say a word any time soon.

'Yes, *tesoro*?' He sat up to bank the pillows, and drew her back up in his arms to lie against them. 'Would you like a drink?'

'In a minute.' She twisted round in his arms, and pushed the hair back from her forehead to look at him, her lips twitching as she saw the utterly blatant male satisfaction on his face. 'Aren't you going to say anything?'

'I love you, *sposa mia*,' he said simply. 'Is there more you would like me to say?'

'You know there is,' she said crossly, then gave a squeak as he pulled her down to him and kissed her long and hard.

'*Va bene.* Then I will say *why*?' he said breathlessly when he released her.

She eyed him narrowly. 'Why did I let you make love to me, or why hadn't I done it before?'

Francesco turned on his back, keeping her sprawled on top of him, his hands smoothing down her spine and over the curves of her bottom. 'I am human and male enough to hope that you did not want to make love with any man except me. Is that true?'

'If it is, I never let myself believe it,' she said bluntly. 'I admit I've never felt the same physical response to any man that I felt for you, but I had another reason for shying away from actual sex—I'm supposed to be divorced.' She gave a little shiver. 'So, although there's been the usual kissing and touching and so on, I never went the distance with a man because it would have raised awkward questions I had no intention of answering.'

Francesco's arms locked around her in sudden, fierce possession. 'And I thank God for it,' he said huskily, his eyes smouldering up into hers. 'You are mine, Alicia. From that first day in Firenze you were mine. You cut me to the heart when you ran from me. All that terrible, endless time I was trying to find you, it was torment to think of you with some other man.'

'And now you know I never was—at least, not like this!' She kissed him to make her point, then drew back, looking down into his intent eyes. 'What is it?'

'You kissed me.'

'So? There was a lot of kissing just now, too.'

'Ah, but I kissed *you*.'

'I soon joined in.'

'*Daverro.*' He stroked a caressing hand down her cheek. 'But I will treasure this little kiss, because it is the first you give of your own accord.'

'True. I could kiss you again if you like,' she offered.

His smile flipped her heart over. 'Ah yes, *amore*, I like very much.'

Alicia discovered that one kiss led straight to another, and the kisses led to caresses which grew so feverish that their positions were soon reversed and Francesco was poised over her again, his face taut with desire.

'I want you again so much, *carissima*,' he whispered, his breath hot against her cheek.

'Then love me again.' She smiled into his possessive eyes. 'Once isn't enough.'

'A thousand times will not be enough!' Francesco held her face between his hands. 'So that I do not hurt you again, I will try to be gentle.' He breathed in sharply as her questing fingers tested his readiness. 'But it will not be easy if you do that!' He moved between the thighs that were already parted for him, and Alicia gave a relishing little purr as Francesco entered her, and with all the skill at his command made love to her again. He was careful, and maddeningly slow at first, but the fierce nature of Alicia's response soon caused acceleration to a fast, glorious rhythm that brought them both to such a heart-stopping orgasm, they stayed clasped tightly together afterwards, Francesco's face buried in her hair.

CHAPTER TEN

ALICIA woke to the unfamiliar feel of a man's arms round her and a chin rough with stubble grazing her cheek.

'*Buongiorno*,' said Francesco in her ear. 'How do you feel today?'

She pushed her hair back and twisted round to meet his eyes, blinking in the sunlight. 'Last night was no dream, then.'

'It was *perfetto*,' he said softly, and kissed her nose. 'You took me to heaven, *diletta mia*. Was it the same for you?'

'Yes.' She buried her face against his shoulder. 'The perfect cure for bad dreams.'

Francesco sighed as he pulled her closer. 'I would give much to stay here and hold you in my arms all day, *carissima*, but we must be ready soon for Signor Raimondi.' He turned her face up for his kiss, then with reluctance slid out of bed.

'What time is it?' she asked, her eyes appreciative as Francesco, splendidly nude, made for the bathroom.

'Nine-thirty. We must hurry. I will run a bath for you while I have a very quick shower.' He smiled over his shoulder. 'But do not wet your hair, *amore*. You must eat breakfast before *il notaio* comes. We have no time for the hairdressing.'

When he emerged, wrapped in a towel, Alicia was standing by the bed, frowning.

'*Che cosa?*' he asked quickly.

She pointed wordlessly to the sheet.

Francesco eyed it with such satisfaction, Alicia suffered one of the rare blushes her pale complexion ever displayed.

'In older, more primitive times I would have hung it from the tower in triumph, as proof to all of my bride's purity!' he informed her triumphantly.

'Barbarian!' She shied a pillow at him. 'That's no help. What do I do about it now, today?'

'Nothing,' he said, catching the pillow with one hand. 'Teresa will change the bed later.' He tossed the pillow down and pulled her in his arms to kiss her. 'Do not be embarrassed, *tesoro*. Your husband feels great joy at so miraculous a gift,' he whispered.

Eyelashes suddenly damp, she kissed Francesco back, then gave him a push when his arms tightened. 'We're late as it is, and I still haven't had my turn in the bathroom.'

He released her reluctantly '*Va bene*—do not be long.'

Alicia eyes were dreamy as she soaked in hot, scented water. Francesco had obviously taken it for granted that Jason Forrester had been her lover, and that there had been others before him— a common misconception in the male-dominated circles she moved in. She smiled at the thought of Francesco's euphoria at finding he was her first lover after all. Just as he should have been all those years ago.

Alicia got out of the bath at last, wincing as various body parts unused to last night's activities protested. She did her face, got dressed quickly in the linen skirt of the night before, and added one of her mother's gifts—a thin ribbed-silk cardigan and v-necked sweater in a burnt-rose shade which, according to Bron the style guru, gave a glow to her daughter's skin and blended, rather than clashed, with her hair. Alicia nodded as she eyed the result. Her mother was right—as usual. She slid the beautiful diamond ring on her finger, and went downstairs to find Francesco on the *loggia* with Giacomo hovering.

'What would you like, *cara*?' asked her husband, holding her chair for her.

'One of these lovely rolls,' said Alicia, and with a smile asked Giacomo for tea.

'You look so beautiful, so elegant—very much *la contessa* this morning, Alicia,' said Francesco, when they were alone. *'My contessa,'* he added. His eyes held hers. 'You are mine, no?'

She looked at him steadily. 'You mean because of what happened last night?'

'It was the most magical experience of my life, it is true,' he agreed. 'But to me you have always been mine.' He leaned nearer to kiss her, unembarrassed when Giacomo interrupted with their breakfast tray.

Alicia found she was ravenous. She downed a glass of orange juice and ate two rolls with butter, and had to use will power to refrain from eating a third while Francesco outlined his plan for the day.

'This morning we spend with Signor Raimundi. Afterwards we lunch with Zia and Bianca, then this afternoon you rest, because this evening I am taking you out to dine.'

Her eyes widened. 'Really? Where?'

'Here in Montedaluca, in a restaurant which opened only last year. It is very popular. I was fortunate to get a table.'

Alicia laughed. 'Oh, come *on*, Francesco. If the Conte da Luca wants a table, there'll always be one available!'

'I cannot say, though it is true I have not been refused. For tonight I asked for the best table for two.' Francesco smoothed a finger over the back of her hand as he smiled into her eyes. 'I wish to show my beautiful wife off to the world. So that all know we are together again.'

Alicia held the brilliant blue gaze steadily. 'Is this because of last night, too?'

'It will be good to *celebrate* last night,' he agreed. 'But I asked for the table as soon as you agreed to come back, *tesoro*.'

She smiled at him so radiantly Francesco leaned nearer, as though pulled with a rope, then with a muttered curse drew away again as Giacomo appeared to ask if they needed anything more.

'Where do we talk to Signor Raimundi?' asked Alicia as they left the *loggia*.

'In my *studio*.'

'Give me five minutes to make repairs and I'll be with you.'

'Be quick!'

Alicia not only obeyed but ran back downstairs in her rush to get back to Francesco. She was as much in love with him as ever. Probably more. Was this just because he'd introduced her to the joy—and it had been joy—of sex? Yet it had not been purely physical. The tenderness and skill underlying Francesco's passion had made the experience magical for her.

'You would never let me in here last time,' she reminded him when Francesco closed the study door behind her.

'And I have told you why! I was hiding from you.'

'Coward,' she teased.

'No, just noble,' he said piously, then gave her a pulse-quickening smile. 'If I had let you come in here I would have laid you down on that desk and ravished you.'

Alicia eyed the carved, beautiful desk with interest. 'Would you, really?'

'I would have wanted to.' Francesco advanced on her with purpose. 'I want to now.'

Alicia backed away, not at all sure he was joking. 'A fine thing if *il notaio* came in to find us making love in the middle of the morning.'

Francesco took her in his arms. 'He is a man, also Italian— he would approve!'

'Oh would he, indeed?' Alicia reached up to kiss him lightly, then backed away. 'No more of that, or my hair will unravel.'

He gave her a glittering, explicit look. 'I like it unraveled.'

Alicia shook a reproving finger at him. 'I've just put it tidy, to impress Signor Raimundi, so hands off, please.'

He slowly released her. 'For now I will obey. But,' he warned, eyes gleaming, 'we shall return to the subject later.' He pulled up a chair close to his own. '*Allora*, sit here with me behind the desk. We shall face Signor Raimundi together.'

'I'm nervous,' she told him.

'Of *il notaio*?'

'No. Of finding out what your mother left me.'

His eyes darkened. 'Forget the other gift that tore us apart. I swear to you, Alicia da Luca, that I will let nothing part us again.' Francesco raised her hand to kiss the ring he'd put on her finger, then looked up at a knock on the door. '*Avanti.*'

'Signor Raimundi,' announced Giacomo. He ushered in a slim, dark-suited man and then withdrew, closing the door behind him.

'*Buongiorno*, Eduardo,' said Francesco, smiling as he got up. 'Allow me to present my wife.'

The notary bowed over the hand Alicia held out to him. '*Piacere, contessa.*' He turned to shake Francesco's hand, formal greetings were exchanged, and when they were all seated he put on his spectacles and opened his briefcase.

'*Mi dispiaci*, but I'm afraid my Italian isn't good enough to understand legalities, Signor Raimundi,' warned Alicia.

He gave her a rather shy, charming smile. 'Then I will speak English, contessa, though alas, not well.'

'No matter.' Francesco took Alicia's hand. 'If necessary I shall be interpreter.'

'*Grazie.*' The lawyer took an envelope and a long package from his briefcase. 'La Contessa Sophia da Luca made me swear to give these personally into your hands,' he said slowly, and slid both across the desk to Alicia. He paused, obviously choosing his words with care. 'She stipulated that you must be here in person in Montedaluca to receive them.'

Alicia put the package aside and examined the envelope, which was addressed to *La Contessa Alicia da Luca*. She looked up at the lawyer as Francesco's grasp tightened comfortingly on her free hand. 'You need me to open these now in front of you?'

'No no, *contessa*, that is not necessary. I have delivered the items to you, therefore I need only your signature and my work is done.' He handed her a thick document, embossed with the name of his firm.

She took a pen from a silver tray on the desk, and, with a look at Francesco, wrote *Alicia Cross da Luca* where the notary indicated then handed the document back. '*Grazie.*'

'*Prego, contessa.*'

Alicia tugged free of Francesco's hand and rose to her feet. 'Now will you have some coffee, Signor Raimundi?'

'That would be most pleasant, *contessa*,' he said courteously.

'Giacomo will have it ready on the *terrazzo.*' Francesco got up to open the door for her. 'But, if you wish to open your letter alone, we understand, *carissima.*'

'Thank you.' She gathered up the letter and package, and preceded the men out into the hall. 'In that case, I think I'll take these up to our room, darling.' She held out her hand to the lawyer. 'Thank you for coming, Signor Raimundi.'

'It was my pleasure, *contessa*. Also a privilege to meet you.' He bowed over her hand.

'*Grazie.*' Alice gave him a friendly smile. '*Arrivederci.*' She turned away to mount the curving staircase, and found that the bedroom was already immaculate with fresh linen on the bed.

Alicia sat on the chaise under the windows and removed wrappings, to reveal a long, leather box. Taking in a deep, unsteady breath, she pressed a button to open it, then sat very still, gazing at a single string of pearls with a diamond-studded clasp. But what pearls! They were natural, baroque pearls, perfectly matched only in size. No two were the same shape. The *contessa* had worn them constantly, except for the day she'd waved her son and his bride off on their honeymoon—the last time Alicia had ever seen her.

Alicia closed the box gently, then opened the envelope. It contained two sheets of paper, one of them labelled, 'to be read first'. It was dated the day after the wedding, in the same copperplate as the name on the envelope. Sophia da Luca had written in the formal English learned from nuns as a schoolgirl, and later, in her aim to be a polished hostess, practiced diligently during daily conversation lessons with Bianca Giusti.

My Dear Alicia,
I regret that I have not welcomed you more warmly, but I have never found it easy to show warmth, except to my beloved Ettore, and to my son Francesco.

To be truthful, you are not the bride I would have chosen for my son. But, because you are his choice, you and I must learn to live together in harmony for his sake. This will be not be easy for you, when you enjoy so close a relationship with your own mother. But now you are Francesco's wife in the eyes of God I will strive to make life happier for you here at the *castello*. The enclosed necklace is my personal bride-gift to you, Alicia. I hope you will wear it with the pleasure it has given me since the day I received it from Ettore, to celebrate Francesco's birth.
With my good wishes,
Sophia da Luca.

Alicia blinked away tears as she finished reading. The letter had obviously been enclosed with the pearls she'd never received. She laid the letter on top of the box and unfolded the other sheet.

My Dear Alicia,
I do not know if Francesco will ever find you, or even if he does that you will come back to Montedaluca to receive this. I pray constantly that you will return, and so learn the truth. Instead of giving this gift into your hands myself, to my eternal regret I entrusted Cinzia, my maid, to deliver it to you while you were packing. I believed she had done so because you thanked me so prettily for my gift.

But soon after you left Giacomo learned that Cinzia had told one of the other maids she was leaving the *castello* that very day. He was suspicious, and asked me to give Cinzia some task that would keep her by my side long enough for him to search her room. Giacomo soon found the pearls hidden among her belongings in a suitcase already packed for her departure. The silly girl had even kept my letter.

Cinzia became hysterical when threatened with the police. She needed to sell the pearls for money to get married, and gave you a pretty nightgown instead, she sobbed. Her tears did not move me. She had expected her crime to remain undiscovered because she would be gone long before you returned. I relented about the police to avoid scandal, but commanded her to leave the *castello* at once. Next day Francesco returned from Paris in such anguish, Alicia, that I forgot Cinzia in my desperate worry about you.

Since you are reading this I pray that the breach is now healed between you and my beloved son. I hope that you will accept the pearls, and wear them with my sincere good wishes.
Sophia da Luca.

Alicia sat for a long time, reading and rereading both letters. She sighed deeply as she returned them to the envelope. So the mystery was solved at last, and she had taken possession of the legacy she'd sworn she wouldn't keep. But that was when her feelings towards both Francesco and his mother were still hostile. Now everything had changed. It was too late for a warm relationship with the *contessa*. But not with Francesco.

She looked up, blinking away tears as Francesco came in. He crossed the room swiftly to sit beside her, an arm round her waist. 'You are sad, *tesoro*?'

Alicia nodded wordlessly. 'You mother left me her pearls. Read the letters, Francesco.'

His face was grim as he finished reading. 'I could murder the girl!'

'Me too,' she agreed fervently. 'As well as money for the pearls, she obviously wanted to ruin our wedding night out of spite because you rejected her. But she never knew how spectacularly well she'd succeeded.'

'Giacomo told me she left town as soon as my mother dismissed her from the *castello*. She has not been heard of since.'

Alicia opened the leather box to show him the pearls. 'You know these so well; would it be painful to see me wear them?'

He shook his head, smiling. 'It would give me great pleasure. Wear them tonight for me.' He got up, drawing her with him. 'Come; Eduardo has gone, and it is nearly time for lunch. Zia and Bianca are already on the *terrazzo*.' He touched his fingers to her cheekbones. 'Your tears have washed your freckles clean.'

She pulled a face. 'You go on, then. I'll just sort my face out before I join you.'

Francesco took her in his arms and kissed her, moving his lips from her mouth to her cheeks. 'You may comb your hair or put on the lipstick, but nothing on the freckles—*per favore*,' he added belatedly.

'All right, you tyrant,' she sighed, resigned, as she went to the dressing table.

'Never tyrant,' he said quickly, and followed her to slide his arms round her to look over her shoulder into the mirror. 'If you wish to cover the freckles, do so, *innamorata*.'

Alicia twisted round in his arms and buried her face against his chest. 'You don't play fair,' she muttered, weak at the knees because 'sweetheart' sounded so much more passionate in Italian.

They stood together, holding each other tightly—Francesco because it satisfied something primitive and possessive in his psyche to hold her close, protected against the world, Alicia because she needed the comfort of physical contact after the emotion of the morning. She drew back at last and smiled brightly.

'Give me a few minutes and I'll follow you.'

His eyes softened. *'Va bene.'*

Alicia held a handful of wet tissues held to her eyes until she was sure her tears were finished, then tidied her hair and put on lipstick, made a face at the undisguised freckles, and went off to join the others on the *terrazzo*.

Zia Luisa and Bianca greeted her with smiles that Alicia returned with warmth, which included Francesco when he gave her freckles an approving look as he seated her at the table.

'How are you, *cara*?' said Luisa with sympathy. 'Was it a difficult morning for you?'

'Not as much as I expected, Zia.' Alicia helped herself to mozzarella-and-tomato salad dressed with olive oil, and basil freshly picked from Antonio's herb garden. 'Signor Raimundi made it surprisingly easy.'

'He is a charming man,' agreed Bianca. 'And most efficient. We received our legacies from the *contessa* very quickly.'

Alicia's fork stopped halfway to her mouth. 'You've already received them?'

Zia Luisa nodded placidly and sipped her wine. 'Sophia was most generous. She forgot no one, not even young Teresa.'

Alicia turned, very slowly, to look at Francesco. 'So I was the only one outstanding?'

'*Davverro,*' he agreed, smiling and unrepentant as he refilled Luisa's glass. 'Only you, Alicia.'

'What did you receive, *cara*?' asked Luisa.

'The *contessa* left me her pearls, Zia.'

'Ettore's pearls?'

'So she said in a letter, yes.'

'How wonderful,' said Bianca. 'With your complexion they will suit you perfectly, Alicia. Though you must be careful to wear a hat in the sun. Already you have freckles again.'

'She has always had them,' said Francesco, and placed a buttered roll on Alicia's plate. 'She hides them now with cosmetics.'

'But why, child?' protested Luisa. 'They are most charming.'

'I keep telling her so,' said Francesco. 'Eat, Alicia.'

She bit into the roll obediently, postponing confrontation with her overbearing husband until later. 'I mustn't eat too much, because Francesco's taking me out to dinner tonight,' she told the ladies, who smiled in fond approval.

'To the new *trattoria*,' agreed Bianca. 'He took us there to celebrate the *signora*'s birthday. It was a delightful meal. Though Pina does just as well,' she added loyally.

'Wear the pearls, *cara*, and when you are dressed you must come and show yourself to us,' said Luisa, smiling. 'See that Alicia rests this afternoon, Francesco.'

'I shall insist that she does,' he assured her.

A dish of baked peaches followed for dessert, after which Luisa's second glass of wine had again left her semi-comatose in her chair.

'I will take the *signora* to her room,' said Bianca softly.

'I'll go with you,' said Alicia, smiling sweetly at Francesco. 'You stay and drink your coffee while I have this rest you insist on.'

Smiling defiantly at Francesco, she took one of Zia Luisa's arms while Bianca took the other.

The old lady came fully awake with a start once she was moving, and smiled sleepily. '*Madonnina*! I must drink only one glass of wine in future.'

'Why?' said Alicia. 'If you enjoy two glasses, what does it matter?'

'You mean at my age?'

'I mean that at your age you're entitled to do exactly what you want.' Alicia grinned cheekily as they reached the tower where Bianca and Luisa slept. 'But then, I fancy you've always done that, Zia, haven't you?'

A veined hand loaded with rings patted her cheek. 'I have indeed, child. Now, rest.'

'Will do. *Ciao*, ladies.' Alicia strolled off along the gallery to the other tower, half expecting Francesco to intercept her. Rather deflated when she reached their room alone, she washed her face and stripped down to knickers and bra and got into bed with a yawn, finding she wasn't really averse to the rest Francesco had insisted on. Tyrant! She snuggled down in the bed, then shot upright again as the door opened and Francesco stalked in with a look in his eye which made his intention clear. Without a word he stripped off his clothes, flung them on the chaise under the windows and got into bed.

'We rest together,' he informed her, and pulled her close. 'Even though you are angry with me.'

'You can hardly be surprised,' she said unevenly. Sharing a bed with a naked man was even more breathtaking in the full light of afternoon. 'All that talk about people waiting for their legacies! You got me back to Montedaluca by false pretences, Francesco da Luca.'

'*Davverro*, Alicia da Luca,' he agreed, in a tone which sent a shiver down her spine. 'But I feel no guilt, only triumph that my plan worked.' He raised her face to his. 'Are you very angry?'

She sighed. 'No. You're a smooth-talking devil, Francesco da Luca.'

'Not devil! Francesco was a saint.' He kissed her with sudden passion. 'But I am not. I am a man.'

'Does that mean you want to make love to me?' Though held so close to him, Alicia had no need to ask.

'No,' he said, startling her, and kissed her again, his inciting hands moving over her back in caresses that moulded her closer. 'I want to make love *with* you. I have enough command of English to make this clear, no?'

'Command is exactly right, Francesco,' she agreed breathlessly.

'Why do you say my name so much?' he demanded. 'I prefer what you said this morning.'

Alicia thought for a moment, then smiled. 'Darling?'

'*Esattamente*.' He lifted her chin to rain kisses all over her face. 'You have not said this to me before, even when we first met.'

'It's not a term I use. Except to you, apparently,' she added, and caught her breath, her eyes wide as Francesco suddenly pulled back the covers and knelt over her to render her as naked as himself.

'I wish to see all of you as we make love,' he told her, and smiled possessively. 'Do not be shy, *amore*. I am your husband, remember?'

'You're a hard man to forget,' she assured him.

He let himself down beside her, turning her in his arms. 'Did you try hard, Alicia?'

'Oh yes.' She leaned into him with a sigh. 'For years I tried. I had even begun to think I'd succeeded. Then I saw you again that day at the stadium and knew I'd forgotten nothing at all.'

'For which I thank God.' He kissed her with mounting passion and she responded with an ardour he delighted in, his eyes alight with the joy of possession as he caressed every curve of her body with his eyes before he began the same process with skilled, importuning hands, and hot, possessive mouth that smothered her gasps with engulfing kisses when his searching caresses found that she was more than ready for him.

Alicia pushed at his broad shoulders, and instantly Francesco raised himself slightly, then groaned like a man in mortal pain as she captured his erection in caressing hands.

'*Dio!*' he gasped. 'No more.' He caught her hands and drew in a deep, unsteady breath, then kissed her and positioned himself between her thighs. 'It will not hurt this time,' he said huskily.

She licked the tip of her tongue round her parted lips. 'Show me, then.'

He grasped her hips, tilted them up to him and slid home into the hot, tight sheath that closed round him in ecstatic welcome.

'*Francesco!*' gasped Alicia. 'I never knew—'

'For which I give thanks,' he said against her lips as he began to move. 'Now, *diletta mia*, we find paradise together.'

CHAPTER ELEVEN

LATER, wearing the fabulous pearls with her pale, filmy dress, Alicia told Francesco the only thing missing was the red carpet as they walked down to the car to drive the short distance into the town. He smiled as he helped her into the car, and assured her she outshone any celebrity beloved of the paparazzi.

At La Taverna da Monte the keys of the Lamborghini Gallardo were entrusted to a youth who received them with due reverence.

'Guido is the son of the owner, Mario Ponti, and plays at outside half for Montedaluca,' Francesco told Alicia. 'He is most promising. He will also take great care of the car.'

'I hope so. It's a beauty!'

'It is you who are the beauty,' he whispered, as a smiling man greeted them at the restaurant door with a flood of Italian so enthusiastic, most of it went straight over Alicia's head.

'Slowly, Mario, slowly,' said Francesco, 'So I may present my beautiful English wife.'

'*Contessa*,' said the man, bowing. 'Welcome. I work many years in England.'

Alicia smiled warmly, expressing interest, which prompted a stream of reminiscences about Oxford and Bath as Mario led them to a table screened with greenery at the far end of a dining room decorated in bright, contemporary style which contrasted vividly with the venerable building which housed it. Every table in the restaurant was full, and, sensing her tension, Francesco kept a protective hand lightly at Alicia's waist as they made their way past diners who greeted him with smiles and waves as they passed.

Mario seated her with a flourish, and Francesco moved his chair close to Alicia, shielding her slightly from the room.

'Thank you,' she whispered as Mario left them to study menus. 'I feel like the cabaret.'

'People here are naturally curious about my companion,' he agreed, pouring mineral water into her glass. 'Now, tell me what you would like to eat and I will choose some wine, *cara*.'

'I rather fancy some fish. What do you suggest?'

'When Mario comes back, we shall ask him.'

They were told that the head chef recommended a dish from his native Livorno. *Cacciucco*, a fish and seafood soup with herbs and tomatoes, would be served over garlic-scented toasted bread. 'The fish is straight from Porto Santo Stefano today,' Mario assured them, and kissed his fingers. 'It is good.'

'It sounds wonderful,' Alicia agreed, and slanted a smile at Francesco. 'Will you mind if I eat garlic?'

He chuckled. 'No, because I shall share your *cacciucco*. And with it we shall drink some Montedaluca Classico, Mario.'

'*Va bene*. Guido will bring it at once.' The man beamed. 'And Carlo will be much honoured that *la Contessa* has chosen his signature dish, as your chefs say in England.'

The *cacciucco* was delicious, as promised, but so filling Alicia could not be tempted to a dessert. And over coffee she began to feel the effects of a day where the emotional revelations of her legacy had been followed by a passionate interlude in bed. 'I'm a bit tired, Francesco,' she confessed.

'Then let us go home.'

Conscious that eyes followed them as they took their leave, Alicia asked Mario to inform the chef that his signature dish was superb, then got into the car as young Guido held the door for her, and waved as Francesco drove away.

'How do you think I did on my first unofficial engagement as your *contessa*?' she asked Francesco.

'You were perfect. All the women admired your dress, and all the men envied me,' he said with satisfaction, and touched a hand to hers. 'For several reasons I am a very happy man tonight. *Grazie*, Alicia.'

'*Prego*, Francesco.'

As soon as the car turned up to the *castello* the doors opened like magic as Giacomo appeared to greet them and put the car away.

'It is his little treat; he loves to drive the Lamborghini,' said Francesco affectionately as they went inside. '*Allora*, it is very early, so would you like to sit on the *terrazza* for a while, or are you so tired that you must go to bed right away?'

Alicia turned at the foot of the stairs, her eyes very direct on his. 'I want to go straight to bed. Will you come with me?'

'You have need to ask?' He seized her hand to hurry her up the stairs. 'But not to make love again. I shall hold you in my arms while you go to sleep, so there will be no bad dreams tonight, *amore*.'

Alicia gave him a sleepy smile as he opened the bedroom door for her. 'Thank you, darling.'

His eyes lit up. 'Say it again.'

'Darling,' she said softly, and turned her back to him. 'Will you undo my zip?'

'Of course, but I must take great care of this dress. Tell your mother I think you are ravishing in it.' He slid the dress down, held it as she stepped out of it, then ran a relishing gaze over her from head to toe. 'You are even more ravishing without it,' he added huskily, 'But do not tell her that, perhaps.'

Alicia laughed, and hung the dress in the wardrobe. 'I doubt that she'd be shocked.' Later, when they were lying together, gazing at the moonlight silvering the floor, Francesco gave a deep, contented sigh. 'I have been so much longing for this.'

'To sleep with me?'

He nodded, and touched his lips to her forehead. 'To make love is rapture and joy, but just to hold you in my arms as we sleep, Alicia, is a dream come true.'

'For me too.' She wriggled closer with a sigh of pleasure. 'But let's not talk of dreams.'

His arms tightened. 'Do not worry, *tesoro*; if you dream tonight I shall wake you up with a kiss.'

Long after Alicia was asleep Francesco lay awake to savour the sheer pleasure of feeling her boneless and relaxed in his arms. How often he had imagined this. His mouth twisted. So much time wasted. But no more. Now that she had given herself to him at last, he would never let her go. But he must be careful. Alicia was used to living—and sleeping—alone. Also working for a living. She would need occupation once she was here for good. But there were many things she could do to help him, if she wished. To work together as a team would be something he could look forward to with anticipation. A wife experienced in public relations would be a great asset. But, more important than all of that, they would be husband and wife at last, as fate had always intended them to be. And one day, if God was good, they would be parents. He smiled at the thought of babies with curly, coppery hair and blue eyes. Then with a sudden curse he shot out of bed at the sound of sonorous clanging from the *castello* bell. He pulled on his clothes as the clanging gave way to hammering on the ancient main-door, and smiled in reassurance as Alicia struggled upright, her startled eyes like saucers.

'Francesco, who on earth is making all that noise?'

'I will soon find out,' he said calmly. 'Stay where you are, *amore*.'

But she was already sliding out of bed. 'If you go, I go.'

Francesco caught her by the shoulders, shaking his head. 'No. I must see first—*Gran Dio*,' he added as the hammering started again. 'Stay here!'

Ignoring him, Alicia ran for her dressing gown, then opened the door and crept cautiously onto the gallery outside as the hammering started again. She breathed in sharply, appalled as she heard a voice—an all too familiar voice—bellowing for Francesco.

'Let me *in*. I know Alicia's in there. You can't keep her here against her will, you bastard.'

Gareth! Alicia groaned in horror as she went halfway down the stairs to a point where she could watch, unseen, as Francesco put Giacomo aside to open the door and Gareth Davies, wild-eyed and haggard, stormed into the hall.

'I've come for Alicia,' he panted. 'Where is she?'

'*Buona sera,*' said Francesco courteously. He glanced briefly at Giacomo, who swung the great door closed and locked it.

'What the hell—?' Gareth swung round, fists clenched, as ancient bolts thudded home. 'You think you can keep me locked up here too? What have you done with Alicia?'

'She is perfectly safe,' Francesco assured him as Gareth, with murder in his eye, let fly with a blow intended to knock the other man flat. But Francesco da Luca, accustomed to side-stepping big rugby-forwards, dodged the blow, thrust a hard hand flat on Gareth's chest in response—and the uninvited guest, too tired from travelling and pent-up emotion to react quickly enough, lost his balance and sat on the stone floor with a thump Alicia heard with a wince from her vantage point, and ran down to interfere.

She reached the hall as Gareth picked himself up, shook his dazed head, then with a roar started again for Francesco.

'*Gareth Davies*, stop this nonsense at once!' she ordered, in a tone which stopped him dead in his tracks.

He turned, rocking on his feet slightly, then made for her, arms outstretched. 'Thank God! Are you all right, *cariad*? I've come to get you out of here—take you home.'

Alicia felt such affection and pity well up inside her, she had to steel herself to evade his embrace. 'Gareth,' she said firmly. 'I came here of my own free will. And I don't want to go home yet. I'm staying here for the rest of my holiday.' A lot longer than that, actually—like the rest of her life.

His arms fell as he stared at her in outrage. 'What?' He shot a malevolent look at Francesco. 'With *him*?'

'Yes, Gareth. With Francesco.' She shot a look at her glowering husband, who was ominously silent, his temper obviously hanging by a thread. 'We've decided to get back together again.'

'No! Are you mad?' Gareth's haggard face paled. 'Alicia, you can't do this, you belong to me!'

Francesco's eyes blazed. 'You are wrong. Alicia is my wife. And now she has returned to me, I will never let her go.'

Feeling like a bone wrangled over by two angry dogs, Alicia glared at them. 'I *belong* to myself,' she snapped. 'Now, let's stop all this macho nonsense and behave like civilised human beings.'

But Gareth, enraged by Francesco's high-handed declaration, made a rush for him, his intention so obviously to batter him into the ground that Alicia, acting on pure instinct, ran between them to intervene. But Francesco thrust her out of the way and met a knockout punch which would have laid him out cold on the floor if Alicia hadn't leapt to break his fall.

Francesco came round slowly to the sound of his frantic wife imploring him to speak to her. He blinked, dazed, as he looked up into wet, dark eyes wide with fear, and found his head was on Alicia's lap, and he was held close in her trembling arms. To his surprise she was sitting on the hard, stone flags with her back to one of the legs of the long table in the hall, which seemed to be full of people, among them Gareth, on his knees beside them, and Giacomo, standing over him with a look that dared the intruder to move.

'Francesco!' said Alicia frantically. 'Speak to me, darling!'

'What—shall—I say, *amore*?' he croaked.

Gareth let out a shaky breath. 'Are you all right?'

'No, of course he's not all right,' Alicia said crossly. 'You knocked him out!'

Francesco gave an unsteady laugh. 'He only managed that, *carina*, because you distracted me.'

'If you've broken any of his teeth, Gareth Davies,' she warned. 'You pay the dentist's bill.'

Still on his knees, Gareth moved in front of Francesco and held up a finger 'How many?'

'*Uno.*'

Gareth moved the finger, and relaxed slightly when the dazed blue eyes followed it. 'Do you feel sick?'

Francesco thought about it. 'I'm not sure. Did my head hit the ground?'

'No, thank God. Alicia's flying tackle caught you before you landed.'

'So this is why we are sitting on the floor,' said Francesco, smiling up at Alicia, who promptly bent to kiss him in passionate relief, missing the look of sudden, rueful comprehension in Gareth's eyes.

Francesco kissed her back, then smoothed her hair back from her face. 'Do not cry, *carissima*. I am fine. *Allora*, Gareth shall help me up, so that you can get up too.'

With a wry twist to his mouth, Gareth helped Francesco to his feet, then held him by the elbows as he swayed slightly. 'Steady.' He turned to Alicia as Giacomo helped her to her feet. 'I'm sorry about all this, *cariad*. I obviously got the wrong end of the stick.'

Bianca hurried towards them, her face anxious. 'I do not wish to intrude, but the bell startled the *signora*, so I must tell her what happened. But first, are you all right, Alicia?'

'I'm fine.' She smiled at Giacomo. 'Thank you.'

'*Prego, contessa.*'

'Would you like some tea, Alicia?' asked Bianca. 'Pina shall make some for you.'

Alicia suddenly noticed that Pina was there in the hall, looking ready to do battle with the intruder, with Teresa peeping, timid and wide-eyed, behind them. 'I'd love some tea, Pina,' she said, smiling at the woman in reassurance.

'*Subito, contessa,*' she said, and gave a malevolent glare to Gareth as she herded Teresa away.

Francesco put his arm round Alicia, and smiled reassuringly

at Bianca. 'Tell Zia all is well. We shall go somewhere more comfortable to drink the tea. And Signor Davies shall have a brandy while a room is made ready for him.'

Bianca smiled, reassured, and hurried upstairs to report.

'After making such a God-awful fool of myself, I'll be glad of a brandy,' said Gareth, shamefaced. 'But I don't need a room. I booked into the hotel I stayed in when—when—'

'Francesco and I got married,' said Alicia, wobbling slightly.

Francesco picked her up, ignoring both her protests and Gareth's demands to surrender the burden to him. 'Follow me,' he said to Gareth, and made for the morning room to put Alicia down on a sofa. 'Sit quietly *amore*, while I talk with Giacomo.' He shot a look at Gareth. 'Have you eaten?'

'No—but I don't want anything.' Gareth eyed him, embarrassed. 'How do you feel?'

'I am only thankful you pulled your punch to avoid Alicia,' Francesco said wryly, then bent to kiss his wife. 'Do not move. I will be a minute only.'

When they were alone Gareth bent to take Alicia's hand, his dark eyes full of remorse. 'What can I say, *cariad*? I sort of lost it when I finally got to the *castello*. I was a bloody idiot, forcing my way in here like that. You know I wouldn't hurt you for the world.'

'Of course I do. I've always known that,' she said soothingly, and looked at him steadily. 'I couldn't have asked for a better brother.'

His mouth twisted as took in a deep, unsteady breath. 'I hear you. Don't worry—I've got the message. Finally. Francesco's obviously still crazy about you, and you feel the same way about him.'

'Yes. For years I persuaded myself I didn't,' she admitted, and smiled ruefully. 'But the moment I saw him again, I knew I'd never stopped loving him.'

'In spite of what he did?'

'He didn't actually *do* anything, Gareth. We just got our wires crossed at a highly emotional moment, and I was too young and wet behind the ears to cope. So I ran.' She gave him a significant look. 'And, because I never knew he came after me, I believed he didn't care, so I tried to stop loving him and did my best to forget him. Without much success on either count,' she added ruefully.

Gareth heaved a sigh. 'I knew I shouldn't have listened to Bron all those years ago. I always felt you had a right to know he came looking for you.' He got to his feet as Francesco came back, followed by Giacomo carrying a tray laden with tea, coffee, mineral water and, despite Gareth's protests, a platter of *arosto misto* Pina had assembled with cold cuts of roast chicken, lamb, pork and slices of crusty bread.

'Thanks very much—you shouldn't have bothered,' he said awkwardly, but Francesco shook his head as he put a glass of brandy at his elbow.

'No guest goes hungry at the *castello*.'

'I bet you never had one who caused a rumpus like I did,' said Gareth heavily. He brightened as he eyed the food. 'Actually, this looks great. I haven't eaten since breakfast this morning.'

'A good thing you didn't down the brandy first, then,' said Alicia, and smiled at Francesco as he handed her a cup of tea. 'How do you feel?'

'I am fine. How about you, *cara*?'

'I'll be fine, too, after I drink this tea.' She made a face at Gareth. 'You still like using your fists too much.'

Francesco sat beside her. 'It could have been worse. He tried to hold back as you ran between us.'

'But I just couldn't pull the punch entirely. Sorry—it won't happen again.'

'You bet your life it won't,' said Alicia. 'What on earth did you think to gain by killing Francesco?'

'I didn't mean to *kill* him,' he said sheepishly.

'Just to smash my pretty face?' said Francesco slyly, and won a reluctant laugh from Gareth.

'Something like that,' he admitted. 'Though a bit of a bruise on your jaw is the only thing I managed. Which is all to the good, because I got things totally wrong, for which I apologise. I honestly thought she hated you.'

'So did I,' agreed Francesco with feeling.

Gareth eyed him wryly. 'It's obvious she thinks a damn sight differently now.'

'Would you mind,' said Alicia wrathfully, 'Not talking as if I weren't here?'

'*Mi dispiaci,*' said Francesco. 'You would like more tea?'

'Yes, but you stay here on the sofa. I'll pour it.'

Alicia sat very close to her husband while she drank her tea, very much aware that, though Gareth attacked his meal with enthusiasm, he was still troubled about something. She exchanged a significant look with Francesco.

'What is wrong?' he asked, refilling Gareth's glass. 'Something still worries you, no?'

Gareth looked at him, as though about to deny it, then nodded slowly. 'The thing is, I just can't forget the state Alicia was in when she came running back home after the wedding. I don't know what happened between you, and believe me I'm not asking for details. But, because I'm the nearest thing to a brother Alicia's got, before I leave here I need your assurance that you'll never make her unhappy again.'

'I swear—'

'Nothing could—'

Francesco and Alicia spoke in unison, then halted and smiled at each other.

She exchanged a long look with Francesco, who nodded in answer to her unspoken question. 'I've never told anyone what happened, Gareth—not even Meg—so, of course everyone blew it up into some awful crime that Francesco never committed.'

'*Davverro,*' said Francesco darkly, and took her hand. 'Tell him, then, *carissima*. Not to clear my name,' he added hastily, 'But to show Gareth that, although I was a stupid fool, I am not quite the monster he believes.'

Gareth shifted uncomfortably in his seat. 'Not a monster, exactly,' he said gruffly.

'But you wanted very much to beat me up that day in your home.'

'Only at first.' Gareth grinned suddenly. 'Not that I would have had all that much success, apparently. You're pretty handy in a fight.'

'*Grazie*; but not quite handy enough tonight!'

'If you're ready, you two,' said Alicia acidly, 'I'll tell my pathetic little tale.'

As concisely, and with as little emotion as possible, she told the brief, edited story of the misunderstanding, right up to the point that morning where she'd received the *contessa*'s legacy of the pearls with the enclosed letters.

'So, if I had calmed down only minutes sooner that evening in Paris,' said Francesco bitterly, 'I would have gone back to our suite before Alicia left and begged her on my knees to forgive me.' He drew in a deep breath. 'Can you imagine how I felt to find her gone?'

'God, yes!' agreed Gareth. 'The day you came to Blake Street with the *contessa* you looked so terrible, I wanted to tell you then and there that Alicia was safe in Hay with my grandmother. But Bron just wouldn't have it. She made me promise I wouldn't say a word, then or in the future. And when my parents backed her up I had to do as she said. But the *contessa* looked so devastated, I felt awful about it.'

Francesco nodded gravely. 'My mother felt much guilt—convinced she was to blame. But it was I who said the words that drove Alicia away.'

'And if I'd had any sense I'd have just waited until you returned and thrown a few choice words of my own back at you,' said Alicia matter-of-factly, and narrowed her eyes at him. 'I would now, believe me.'

He grinned. 'I do believe you. Perhaps now you would throw more than just words, no?'

'Any missile to hand—so be warned!'

Gareth's eyes were rueful as he looked from one smiling face to the other. 'Look, you two, I really appreciate your telling me something so private.' He grimaced. 'Though I feel like an even bigger fool now over the fuss I made. Incidentally, that's some door-bell you've got here.'

'*Davverro,*' agreed Francesco. 'In the past it was used to summon the people of the town to the *castello* in time of danger, but it has not rung for many years. If you had looked closely, you would have seen a modern bell-press by the door.'

'Gosh,' said Alicia, eyes sparkling. 'Will a crowd of people come streaming up here to your defence tonight?'

'I think not. The custom has long since been forgotten,' Francesco assured her. 'But, no matter. If someone comes to make sure all is well, Giacomo will explain.'

'That I went berserk?' said Gareth ruefully.

Francesco shook his head, grinning. 'My faithful Giacomo will say we were having the fire drill.'

'Do you do that often?' asked Alicia.

He shrugged. 'There is always a first time.' He looked up at a knock on the door. 'Avanti.'

Giacomo came in, and with a bow to Alicia surprised her by speaking to Francesco in careful, heavily accented English. 'I informed the hotel that Signor Davies sleeps here tonight. Teresa has prepared the room used by the *contessa.*'

'*Grazie*, Giacomo,' said Francesco. 'We need nothing more tonight. Unless you would like more tea, *carina*?' he said to Alicia.

She shook her head and smiled at the small, neat man. '*Grazie*, Giacomo.'

He bowed, smiling, picked up the tray, wished them goodnight, and went out.

'You're a high-handed lot,' said Gareth dryly, and eyed his half-empty brandy glass. 'Thanks—I didn't fancy driving back down to the hotel tonight.' He grimaced. 'But I wish you'd put me somewhere less grand than the *contessa*'s room!'

Francesco laughed. 'Giacomo meant Alicia's old room. My wife is *contessa* now.'

'Hallelujah, so she is.' Gareth got up and swept Alicia a mocking bow. 'Is Your Highness feeling better now?'

'Yes, I am—but any more of that and *you* won't be,' she retorted, scowling.

Gareth was suddenly very sober. 'Look, just so you both know, I'll never say a word, I promise.'

'I know that,' Alicia assured him, and exchanged a look with her husband. 'Actually, since we're going to have another shot at our marriage—'

'One which will succeed this time,' said Francesco with supreme confidence.

'It had better, after all this trouble,' she said wryly. 'But the people who matter deserve to know what went wrong last time. I could never even tell Bron before, because I thought—and I apologise humbly to her memory—that the tacky gift which caused the trouble came from the *contessa*. But she left me the legacy of truth along with her pearls, so I want everyone to hear it. You agree, Francesco?'

'I do,' he said positively, and sighed impatiently. 'If you had known this truth sooner, we could have been reconciled years ago. I was an arrogant fool. I should have ignored my pride and continued searching for you.'

'Yes, you should,' she said tartly. 'As I said before, I wasn't in hiding.'

'You could hardly blame him for giving up when for years you kept on refusing to have anything to do with him,' put in Gareth.

Alicia rolled her eyes. 'You've changed your tune!'

He shrugged. 'Just trying to be fair.'

'That's rich, when you tried to kill Francesco earlier on.'

He shrugged uncomfortably. 'I didn't have all the facts then.'

'I will return to Cardiff with Alicia, and we shall tell our story together so that *all* may know the facts,' said Francesco firmly, and looked down into her pale face. 'And now, *contessa*, I think you should be in bed.'

'He's right, Lally,' said Gareth, and smiled crookedly at Francesco. 'You look as if a lie down wouldn't go amiss too.'

'Which is hardly surprising,' Francesco retorted, fingering his jaw.

Alicia got to her feet, ignoring both pairs of hands outstretched to help her.

'After crushing you, it is only fair I carry you,' said Francesco firmly, but Alicia waved him away.

'If you gentlemen walk upstairs either side of me, I'll be fine,' she assured him. Even if Francesco could manage the feat in his present condition, it would be asking too much of Gareth to see her carried off to bed in her husband's arms.

CHAPTER TWELVE

NEXT morning Alicia longed to give in when Francesco tried to persuade her to stay in bed. Instead, she showered, dressed in jeans and T-shirt, and ignored Francesco's protests as she used her concealing cream on his bruised jaw instead of her freckles.

'Luckily my bruises don't show,' she told him. 'I sat down with a bit of a thump when I broke your fall.'

'For which I am most grateful.' He slid a caressing hand over her bottom. 'I shall look forward to kissing your bruises better.'

She grinned in such open delight at the idea he caught her to him and kissed her hard.

'*Ti amo,*' he whispered.

They went out on the *terrazzo* to join their guest for breakfast, where discussion centred on Francesco's promising local rugby-club, and the success rate of the club Gareth played for. When he got up to leave, with reiterated thanks and apologies, Alicia kissed Gareth's cheek, sent her love to his parents, and then stood with Francesco at the great door to wave him on his way.

'Now, *sposa mia*, you go back to bed,' said Francesco in a tone which told her not to argue.

'But I'm fine—it's you who should be in bed.'

'And I shall be, this afternoon. With you,' he promised, kissing her. 'But you had a shock last night. You need a rest.'

'Just until lunchtime, then.' She yawned. 'I had to get up this morning, otherwise Gareth would have been in an even worse state of remorse.'

'*Davverro*. Gareth said this to me when you went to see Bianca and Zia Luisa. He also asked us to keep his visit secret from his family,' Francesco informed her as they went slowly upstairs. 'They have no idea that he decided to come here.'

'Oh Lord!' Alicia groaned. 'And he didn't tell me that, because he knew I'd argue. I'm so tired of secrets, Francesco.' She eyed him hopefully as they reached their room. 'Do I really have to go to bed?'

The look Francesco gave her silenced her as he turned the covers back. 'Do this to please me, *innamorata*.'

Because she could resist neither the smile nor the endearment—and she really liked the idea anyway—Alicia meekly took off her shirt and jeans and slid under the covers to lean back against the pillows Francesco had piled ready. 'Won't you stay with me, darling?'

Francesco bent to kiss her. 'Do not tempt me. I will report to Zia and Bianca that I am unharmed, then come back later. *Allora*; is there more you need?'

She tried a coaxing smile. 'I've got some books in my holdall.'

He shook his head. 'No reading. Sleep.'

'Oh, very well,' she sighed, and wagged an admonishing finger. 'But don't expect to get your way every time, *Signor Conte*.'

He laughed and bent to kiss her again. 'I would so much like to stay here with you, but I have certain arrangements to make. Now rest.'

The arrangements Francesco made were to delegate his workload to the staff who manned his offices in the town, so that for the remainder of Alicia's holiday he could spend every moment possible with his wife, leaving her only when she rang her mother or Meg for a chat, or took the daily Italian lesson she insisted on with a delighted Bianca. Francesco drove Alicia down into the town to shop for gifts to take home, took her on a tour of his vineyards and the small marble-quarry he owned, and also to the small, idyllically situated rugby club to meet the young, enthusiastic team.

And on every possible occasion he introduced her to everyone they met, either as *'la mia sposa'* or *'la mia Contessa'*, as appropriate—both of which gave Alicia a terrific buzz, she confided to Francesco in private later. They attended mass with Zia Luisa and Bianca, and short of taking out a notice in the local newspaper Francesco made it very clear to the citizens of Montedaluca that he was reunited with his young wife.

The night before they were due to fly back to the UK there was an air of desperation in Alicia's response to Francesco when they made love. Afterwards, when they lay quiet in each other's arms, he gazed down into her eyes, one hand smoothing her tumbled hair.

'Che cosa, amore?'

'I'm afraid,' she said huskily, and buried her face against his chest.

'Afraid? Of what, Alicia?'

'That when we leave here something will go wrong.' She caressed his hard, muscular chest as she raised her head. 'I know it's illogical, but here in the *castello* it feels like an enchanted world; isolated from everyday life.'

'And once we leave here you think this enchantment will vanish?' He drew her closer when she nodded. 'I have told you, *carissima*, that I will let nothing come between us again. Ever. I swear this to you.' He smiled down at her. 'We have survived attack by Gareth, and told him the truth. He no longer feels *quite* so hostile towards me, and his feelings for you have apparently reverted to brotherly again, thank God. Perhaps once we tell our story to your mother, also to Megan and her parents, they also will not be hostile.'

Alicia was silent for a while in Francesco's embrace, feeling his heart beating against hers. 'My mother will want what I want this time round, so will Meg,' she said quietly at last. 'And I would naturally prefer that everyone wishes us both well, but, even if they don't, nothing will keep me away from you again, Francesco.'

'*Grazie, amore,*' he said huskily, and kissed her in passionate gratitude. 'We have wasted so much time apart, I grudge any minute in future that you are not here with me.'

'Me too. But I'll have to work out my full notice period, plus any extra time needed to show the ropes to my successor,' she said with a sigh. 'But what do I tell people? I'm supposed to be divorced, remember?'

'Tell those you think important that we were just *separato*, and now we are no longer,' he said simply. 'And will never be again,' he added, and kissed her so possessively that she forgot her qualms and surrendered to the joy and heat of a passion she responded to with heart, body and soul. They soared together to such a pinnacle of ecstasy that, after the final wave of sensation engulfed them in climactic bliss, sleep overtook them before they could bear to separate.

The following morning Bianca knocked on their door while Alicia was in the shower to inform Francesco that the *signora* was unwell, and she had taken the liberty of ringing Dr Alva.

'*Bene*, that was most wise,' he said instantly, and smiled reassuringly at Alicia as she emerged, wrapped in a bath towel. 'Zia is not feeling well—her heart gives her trouble sometimes.' He turned back to Bianca. 'She has been taking her medication?'

'Of course, *signore*. I make sure of that.' Bianca smiled ruefully. 'She insists that her little pain is indigestion after indulging too much at dinner last night. But I do not like her colour, and her pulse is fast.'

'You were wise to ring for the doctor,' Francesco assured her.

'You go and see to Zia, darling,' said Alicia anxiously. 'I'll get dressed and finish my packing.'

But by the time they should have been leaving for the airport Zia Luisa was no better, and at last the doctor advised transferring her to the local hospital, at which point Alicia insisted Francesco accompanied his great-aunt.

'Giacomo can drive me to Pisa. You're needed here,' she said firmly. 'You can follow me to Cardiff when Zia is better.'

Francesco held her close. 'I am torn in two pieces,' he said huskily. 'But you are right. I must stay. Ring me as soon as you arrive,' he added. 'I will be at the hospital until I am sure Zia is out of danger.'

Alicia gave in, kissed him quickly, then made a brief visit to Zia Luisa, who lay pale and breathless on her bed, beads of perspiration on her forehead.

'It is so stupid, *piccola*. I do not want the hospital.'

'Best to make sure. Francesco and Bianca will be right there with you.' Alicia bent to kiss the soft, wrinkled cheek. 'I need you in good shape by the time I come back.'

The faded eyes gleamed. 'You are coming back to stay?'

Alicia nodded.

'*Bene*. Come soon. Francesco needs you, Alicia.'

'I need him too, Zia.' Alicia smiled affectionately. 'I must go now if I'm going to catch that plane. So, you be good, please!'

If it was hard to say goodbye to Zia Luisa, it was agony to part with Francesco. They clung together in the hall while Giacomo rushed through a sudden downpour of rain to load the car, then Francesco held an umbrella over Alicia's head while he issued a stream of instructions, and at last installed her in the passenger seat of the Lamborghini. He reminded Giacomo to drive carefully, not for the first time, and to report back to him at the hospital once he had taken the *contessa* to the airport.

'*Si, signore,*' said the man patiently. Giacomo waited, eyes averted, while Francesco kissed his wife again, then as soon as the car door was closed drove off down the steep hill. Alicia sat twisted round in her seat to wave at Francesco, but he was soon obscured by a heavy curtain of rain as lightning flashed and thunder rolled to match her mood.

In a waiting room at the hospital later Francesco paced like a caged lion while his great-aunt was subjected to various tests. He stared at the elements raging outside, praying that Alicia would be safe. He knew of old that she hated storms. The weather could change long before her flight, he assured himself, his spirits rising slightly when the consultant came to inform him that Signora da Luca could go home. Her own diagnosis of indigestion had been correct. She had been given new medication for this, told that in future she must be extra careful with her diet, and limit her intake of the wine she was so fond of. Since there was no immediate danger to her health, and Signora Giusti was able to take care of her, the consultant had surrendered to the *signora*'s pleas to allow her to return to her own bed.

Bianca was desperately guilty for ruining Francesco's plans to travel to Cardiff with Alicia, and begged his forgiveness for the fears which had proved unfounded. But Francesco assured her that she had been right to ring Dr Alva, who, he reminded her, would not have admitted his great-aunt to the hospital unless he had felt it necessary. At her age, chances could not be taken.

Soon afterwards Giacomo arrived back to report that the *contessa* had refused to let him wait until the plane left, worried that her husband might need him.

Francesco, appalled by the idea of Alicia waiting in Pisa alone, forced a smile as Luisa appeared in a wheelchair pushed by a nurse, with Bianca walking alongside. And once back at the *castello*, after a journey which took twice as long as normal due to a hailstorm, Francesco ignored his great-aunt's protests and carried her up to her room. Ordering her to be good, he laid her on the bed, then kissed her lovingly and left her with Bianca—just as the power failed and the *castello* was left without electricity.

He went down to his office to find some paperwork to pass the time, but found it impossible to concentrate as he stared out at the storm, which showed no immediate signs of abating. There was no answer when he rang Alicia's phone. Unable to use his computer, Francesco abandoned all pretence of trying to work and kept trying Alicia's phone. At last he gave up and just sat, willing his own to ring. But when the power came back on it was the main telephone on his desk which rang at last, and he grabbed it with an unsteady hand.

'Alicia?' he said thankfully, wincing at the sound of crackling in his ear.

'Actually, no, it's Bron, Francesco. Bronwen Hughes,' she added, in case he was in any doubt. 'Can you hear me? This line is very bad.'

'Yes, I hear you,' he said, raising his voice. 'We have a storm here. How are you? Has Alicia arrived?'

'That's why I'm ringing. She hasn't yet. I offered George's services as chauffeur to pick her up from the airport, but Alicia said it was all arranged.'

Francesco fought hard against panic. 'I told her to take a taxi. She promised to ring when she landed, but I have heard nothing yet.'

'Neither have I. No doubt she'll get in touch soon. I'd better get off the line so she can contact you.'

'I will tell her to ring you afterwards.'

'Thank you, Francesco. How is your great-aunt, by the way?'

'Much improved. It was indigestion, not her heart, after all. I was able to bring her home, and she is now resting in her own bed.'

'I'm so glad.' A pause. 'I can't help feeling worried about Alicia. You know what mothers are!'

'*Davverro*, none better.' He tried to ignore the cold feeling in the pit of his stomach. 'Bronwen, ring me as soon as you hear from her, *per favore*.'

'Of course I will. Or, if you hear first, you can ring me? If you've got a pen I'll give you my mobile number, and the one here at the house.' She gave a shaky little laugh. 'Now we can communicate.'

If only they had communicated more freely years ago, thought Francesco moodily, a lot of heartache could have been avoided—for both Alicia and himself.

Glad he could now use the computer, he switched it on to check the times of flights from Pisa, and saw much to his relief that, although much delayed by the storm, the flight Alicia was booked on should have already landed in the UK.

But still she had not rung. Francesco felt the cold sweat of fear break out on his neck and trickle down the back of his shirt. His mouth twisted in distaste. He needed a shower. With his phone in his hand, he ran upstairs to the master suite which already felt empty and lonely without Alicia. He hesitated. If he stood in the shower he might not hear her. But he could at least wash and put on a fresh shirt. He put his phone in his pocket and began to sluice water over his head and shoulders. He towelled himself dry and reached for the Aqua Parma lotion he had used all his adult life, his heart contracting as he saw that Alicia had left some of her things behind on the shelf. God, he needed to hear her voice! Then he cursed suddenly in frustration as he spotted a gleam of metal behind her perfume on the shelf—Alicia had left her phone behind.

Feeling queasy from the flight, Alicia was glad she'd had the sense to leave half her belongings behind at the *castello*. She grabbed her solitary holdall from the carousel and made a beeline for the nearest public phone, angry with herself for leaving her mobile behind. Francesco had keyed his own mobile number into it, which meant she had no idea what it was. Thankfully she had the *castello* number in her diary. But Francesco could still be at the hospital. She could at least leave a message to say she'd arrived at last, and he'd get it some time. After waiting out the violent storm in Pisa, the plane had finally taken off through turbulence which had clenched her white-knuckled hands to the arms of her seat, and now, after landing here through more of the same, Alicia needed to be in Francesco's arms like she needed to breathe. She used her credit card to ring the *castello* number, and after waiting for what seemed like forever she heard a husky voice demand, *'Alicia?'*

'Yes, darling. I finally made it; I've just collected my luggage. I couldn't ring before because I left my phone behind. It was a horrible flight, and I was frightened, and I want you so *much*—' To her deep mortification Alicia burst into tears.

'Innamorata!' he said frantically. 'It is agony to hear you cry

when I can do nothing to comfort you. But at least you are safe. I have been mad with worry.'

'Sorry!' She blew her nose on a tissue, and pulled herself together to listen.

'You left your phone in our bathroom. So, now, call your mother *subito*, because she was very anxious when she rang me. Then find a taxi. If the weather is bad, offer the driver any money he wants.'

'Bron rang you? Heavens! But tell me about Zia Luisa—I was afraid you might still be at the hospital.'

Francesco explained briefly. 'Now call your mother, *amore*; I will talk to you later.'

When Alicia arrived in Cowbridge by taxi, after another unpleasant journey through sheeting rain, her reception from Bron was unusually emotional, and even laid-back George Hughes hugged her convulsively and poured her a glass of the Burgundy he kept for special occasions.

'But first ring your husband,' he said, eyes twinkling. 'Bron says he's in a bit of a lather.'

'Sorry to add a call to Italy to your bill, George.'

'Never mind that,' said Bron impatiently. 'Put Francesco's mind at rest. Go into George's den, darling. You can be private in there.'

Alicia gave them both another hug, then raced to shut herself in George's sanctuary. 'Francesco?' she said breathlessly, when he answered. 'I'm here.'

'*Deo gratia!*' he exclaimed, his voice cracking in relief. 'Are you better now, *tesoro*?'

'As better as I can be without you. Sorry I was such a cry baby when I rang, Francesco.'

'Since you cried because you needed me, do not be sorry, Alicia.' He sighed thankfully. 'Now I may even sleep a little tonight—though it will be very lonely in my bed, *amore*.'

'Is Zia well enough for you to come and join me soon in mine, Francesco?'

'I will wait for a day or two to make sure all is well with her, but already she is herself again now she is at home. Bianca is with her, and Pina and Giacomo are ready to do her slightest bidding, so I shall be with you as soon as I can. Now, rest well, *carissima*, and no more crying.'

'Not a tear. But listen, Francesco.'

'I am listening.'

'When you ring back, I have a suggestion to make.'

'Whatever you wish,' he promised her. 'Even if that wish is to keep your job a little longer.'

'Nothing like that,' she assured him. *Quite the opposite.* 'I can't keep George waiting for his dinner any longer, poor thing, so ring me back about ten tonight and I'll tell you about the plan I was hatching while I waited at Pisa.'

'I am impatient to hear it. But I will ring later as you ask. *Ciao, amore.*'

During dinner Alicia told her not very surprised mother that she intended to go back to Francesco, and at long last, years after the event, gave them a watered-down version of the episode that had sent her running home before the ink was dry on her marriage lines.

'Was that all?' said Bron, astonished. 'I imagined far worse.'

'It was just my illusions he damaged,' said Alicia ruefully, and smiled at George. 'You didn't know me then, but I was really wet behind the ears—the most clueless teenager on the planet.'

'My fault for keeping you on such a tight rein,' said her mother with remorse. 'Though to be fair I sent you to the convent school because it had such a good academic reputation.'

'And because you wanted your baby girl in safekeeping with the nuns,' added George gently.

'Well, yes. Because of what happened to me, I was too protective. I realise that now. I was afraid to let her out of my sight right from the start. If I hadn't had Eira to help look after her I would never have gone back to college, let alone held down a job afterwards.' Bron smiled wryly. 'Can you imagine how I felt about letting Alicia go to Florence on holiday without me? And I was right. Look how that turned out!'

'But if I hadn't gone I wouldn't have met Francesco,' Alicia reminded her, and smiled at George. 'Sorry to embarrass you, but I fell in love with him the moment I laid eyes on him. And now that we're back together again it seems as though we've never been apart,' she added, and shivered suddenly.

'What's the matter?' demanded her mother.

'There was so much turbulence on the flight, I was afraid the plane would crash.' She gave her listeners a wry smile. 'It taught me a lesson—life is too short to waste a minute of it. So when I talk to Francesco later I'll tell him about my change of plan.'

When the telephone rang a minute or two short of ten, Alicia excused herself to answer it, in too much of a rush to notice the indulgent smiles that followed her as she shot from the room.

'Francesco?' she said breathlessly.

'*Davverro.* I hope you were not expecting someone else?'

'No. Only you, Francesco. Always.'

He sighed with satisfaction. 'It gives me great pleasure to hear you say this, *innamorata.*'

'I thought it might. Though it's true. How is Zia Luisa?'

'She is back to normal. Poor Bianca is trying to follow the doctor's orders, but Zia is already making life difficult for her about drinking less wine.'

'Oh, poor Zia.' Alicia took in a deep breath. 'Listen, Francesco, I have a plan.'

'It is strange that you should say that, *tesoro*, because I also have a plan. But yours first.'

'I must work my two weeks' notice, but I don't want to work a second longer than that after all.'

'I agree completely, *cara*,' he assured her. 'And now here is my plan, *sposa mia*—I will spend tomorrow arranging everything here so that I can stay with you until you finish your job and are ready to come home to Montedaluca with me. You like my plan?'

Her face lit up like a Christmas tree. 'I *adore* your plan,

Francesco. I just wish you were here right now so I could show you how much!'

'You can show me when I arrive. I shall look forward to this very much.' His voice deepened. 'I went through hell today, Alicia, until I knew you were safe.'

'I wasn't very happy myself,' she said unsteadily, and broke off to blow her nose.

'Which is why I'm against wasting any more time apart. Let me know which plane you're taking and I'll come to meet you at the airport. Would you mind coming here to Bron's for a meal before we go to the flat?'

'I shall be most happy to meet your mother again, also to make your stepfather's acquaintance. But I shall be happiest of all just to be with you again.'

One glimpse of her husband's glossy black curls among the disembarking passengers at Cardiff international airport had Alicia thrusting her way through the crowd like a rugby forward hell-bent on touching the ball down for a try. His eyes lit up, and he dropped his suitcase to sweep her into his arms, swinging her round in jubilation for a moment before he set her on her feet to kiss her.

'Hi,' said Alicia, when she could speak.

'Amore,' he breathed, and kissed her again. He retrieved his suitcase, keeping his free arm firmly around her as they made for the exit. 'We need a taxi?'

'No. I drove.' She smiled up at him. 'First we have lunch with Bron and George, then I drive you to my place. Tomorrow evening we're having dinner with Megan and Rhys, but tonight it's just you and me.'

'Perfetto,' he assured her, his eyes devouring her as they made for the car. 'You look so young today, Alicia; like the teenager I lost my heart to in Firenze.'

Since her aim in wearing jeans and a T-shirt with her hair in a loose braid had been exactly that, she smiled radiantly. 'I thought you'd be pleased.'

The lunch with Bron and George was a great success. The two men took to each other on sight, and Bron's welcome to her son-in-law was so much warmer than their previous encounters he gently teased her about it over the meal.

'You are not angry because I take your daughter away from you again?' he asked later.

Bron shook her head. 'No, Francesco, because that's very obviously what her heart desires.'

He gave Alicia a look that brought a tear to her mother's eye. 'It is what my heart desires also. And this time,' he added very seriously, 'I will take great care to make her happy, Bronwen.'

They lingered over coffee afterwards until at last George took pity on Francesco and suggested the pair resume their journey.

'We can talk longer next time, but you'd better be on your way now to beat rush hour into Cardiff,' he added, with a look at his wife.

'Good thinking, darling,' she said promptly, and hugged her daughter, and then Francesco, as they said their goodbyes.

'I probably won't drive fast enough for you,' Alicia told Francesco once they were on their way.

'Now we are alone together, I am in no hurry,' he said, sitting back, relaxed. 'It is good just to sit here in your little car and enjoy being together again after so long.'

'It was only three days, Francesco,' she said, smiling.

'It felt like three years. Let us have no more partings. We have wasted too much time already, *carina.*'

On the way up in the lift to her apartment, Francesco gave Alicia a wry smile.

'What are you thinking?' she asked.

'I was remembering the first time we did this, *carina*. You were very tense.'

'It was your smell.'

'*Cosa?*' he demanded, appalled.

'You still use the same cologne, or whatever. It brought everything back so vividly, I could hardly breathe,' she confessed as the lift door opened, and smiled at him. 'This time it will be different.'

It was. The moment they were inside the flat Francesco dumped the suitcase and swept her up in his arms to make for the bedroom she'd cleaned and polished the day before in anticipation of just this moment.

'It is time for a siesta,' he said unevenly as he laid her on the bed.

'Yes *please*,' she said, with such fervour he laughed joyously as he began to undress her.

Within seconds they were naked in each other's arms, so on fire for each other that with no preliminaries of any kind they were caught up in the heat and joy of a union made all the more passionate by their brief, but nerve-wracking parting. Francesco told his wife over and over again in two languages how much he loved her.

'We must never be parted again,' he said huskily at last, holding her close. 'Tell me you feel this also, Alicia.'

'Of course I do!' She turned her face up to kiss him. '*Ti amo*, Francesco.'

A fortnight later, after a round of farewell parties, the final, most important celebration of all was held in Blake Street. Eira Davies had begged the privilege of hosting it in the house where Alicia had grown up. And Bron was happy to agree.

'You're a much better cook than I am, Eira, anyway,' she told her friend affectionately. 'Only don't exhaust yourself. It's just the family.'

'She'll have me peeling and chopping for hours,' said Huw gloomily, and grinned at George. 'Fancy lending a hand?'

'I can help also,' offered Francesco, and instead of refusing politely, as Alicia had expected, Eira promptly co-opted him into the all-important business of organising the wine.

'But choosing only, mind, no paying,' warned Eira, patting Alicia's hand. 'We're only too glad to do this for our girl.'

'You are most kind.' Francesco acquiesced gracefully. 'So first we celebrate our reunion here, then soon you must all come back to Montedaluca to stay at the *castello* for another celebration.'

* * *

But, unlike the cosy, comfortable family party in Cardiff, the celebration Francesco had planned in Montedaluca promised to be the event of the year. The town was agog with the news that *il conte* had organised a special charity match at the rugby club he had helped develop to such a standard it now competed in a minor Italian league. The proceeds from ticket sales would provide new equipment for the children's wing of the town's hospital, and the count himself would be playing in a team of veterans composed of friends from his rugby-playing days, and also friends and relatives of the countess. And after the game there was to be a party with a display of fireworks, after a supper provided by Mario Ponti, whose son Guido played in the star position of outside half.

'Amazing place you have here, Francesco,' said David Rees-Jones as Giacomo served drinks on the *castello* terrace the night before the match.

'It is home,' said Francesco simply, his eyes on Alicia, who was laughing with Megan at the sallies of Gareth's teammates. '*Scusi*, David. I think I must rescue my wife.'

'Don't worry, mate, she's used to fending off rugby players.'

'I know all about rugby players,' said Francesco darkly, and grinned. 'I was one myself.'

'And you'd better live up to your reputation tomorrow,' warned David. 'I've been training like a madman since I was idiot enough to say yes to your wife about this.'

'Alicia is very persuasive,' agreed Francesco, smiling at her across the terrace.

'Clever girl all round. We miss her back home—she was great at her job.' With regret David, refused another drink. 'Better keep a clear head. I just hope I'll be in one piece this time tomorrow!'

'Of course you will, *amico*. Come and talk to my great-aunt. Zia Luisa thinks you're very handsome.'

David preened. 'Does she, indeed? She's pretty handsome herself. I bet she was an absolute corker when she was a girl.'

Francesco repeated this to Luisa, who was enjoying herself

enormously, with Bronwen on one side and Eira on the other. She gave David a flirtatious smile as he bowed low before them.

'The Three Graces themselves,' he said reverently. 'Will you be at the match tomorrow, ladies?'

'Wouldn't miss it,' Bron assured him, and smiled at Francesco. 'Eira here can cheer on Gareth, while Luisa and I support my son-in-law.'

'I shall do my best for you, Bronwen,' he assured her. 'I shall leave you ladies with my good friend here, but now I must help Gareth defend Megan and my wife from their admirers!'

'They might not want to be defended,' said Eira sweetly, and grinned naughtily as Francesco scowled.

'Let your wife be, Francesco,' said Luisa placidly, and smiled indulgently at the other women. 'He does not like to let her out of his sight.'

Francesco nodded, unruffled. 'Do you blame me? Ah, Giacomo is having a word with Alicia. I think dinner is about to arrive. It is served early tonight, to make sure all the veterans get to bed early in preparation for tomorrow.'

The following day it was plain from the start that the veteran team was taking the match very seriously indeed. Francesco had seated his family and guests in a special box looking down on the halfway touchline, and from the moment the capacity crowd roared as he jogged onto the field with his team of veterans Alicia felt the same electricity in the air she'd experienced at the match in Cardiff, where they had been reunited.

'Francesco's in very good shape,' commented George. 'Gareth too.'

'Gareth plays regularly, mind, so he should be,' said Huw, eyeing the youthful home team as they came running onto the pitch. 'These lads are a bit lighter than the veterans, but they'll be faster to make up for it.'

Alicia tried to relax, to enjoy the sunshine and the idyllic setting of the small rugby ground, packed today for the occasion. But secretly she was praying that Francesco would not only do well in front of his home crowd for his sake, but manage to avoid any injuries to his person while he was doing it for her own.

'Relax,' murmured Megan, alongside her. 'Your husband looks pretty fit to me.'

Alicia smiled ruefully. 'He trains regularly with the team. Such a pity Rhys couldn't come, Meg. He'd have loved this.'

'I know. But holiday time has left his department short-staffed, so he had to stay behind, poor love.'

'You do realise,' muttered Bron, 'That this is the first rugby match I've ever watched?'

'You'll enjoy it,' her daughter assured her, and grinned. 'And there'll be champagne and gorgeous food at the party afterwards.'

'Why else do you think I came?'

It soon became clear that experience was as valuable an asset in a rugby player as youth, when the old hands began demonstrating their skills. Francesco had delighted Alicia by asking Gareth to captain the team from his position at No.8, in a pack which contained two of his teammates from his rugby club as flankers. David Rees-Jones was playing in the centre as one of a pair with one of Gareth's friends, and the rest of the team was made up of Francesco's former club friends, including the vital half-back pairing.

'Francesco says that Enzo Manetti, the outside half, used to be a miraculous place kicker,' said George, on his feet with Huw as Enzo took a long pass from his scrum half and sent it out to David, who was promptly brought down by three of the opposing team.

'Oops,' muttered Alicia, then heaved a sigh of relief as David jumped up and play resumed.

It was a fast and furious game, so fast that at half time, when the scores were even, some of the veterans were very obviously glad of a breather. Francesco grinned up at Alicia as the teams ran back out to resume play, and she waved back, flushing slightly as she caught Huw's eye.

'Don't worry, *cariad*. He can still run fast enough to stay out of trouble.'

'Not that fast,' she said tightly as two of the opposing forwards sent Francesco crashing to the ground.

'It's all right, Lally,' said Megan. 'He's up and running again.'

The game became more ragged as players, both young and mature, began to tire. Then young Guido made a dash for the line and grounded the ball just out of reach of Gareth's tackle, and the crowd went mad. They were even more vociferous as the ball sailed between the posts from Guido's kick to convert the try, and Montedaluca were seven points ahead. The play immediately surged the other way as the ball went from hand to hand among the veteran three-quarter line, and Enzo Maretti sold a dummy to the man chasing him, did a graceful turn and kicked the ball between the posts for a perfect drop goal, reducing the home team's lead by three. By this time everyone in the crowd, including Francesco's guests, were on their feet as play surged back and forth. Then, in a move so smooth they might have been practising it on the same team for years, Enzo Maretti took a long throw from his scrum half, passed it to David, who sent it winging to Francesco, and Alicia screamed encouragement at the top of her voice as Francesco caught the ball and ran like the wind towards the line, sidestepping and evading his opponents on the way. He snatched a look to see if he had support, saw Gareth frantically waving him on, and made a final spurt which landed him over the line with arm outstretched to ground the ball, his smile unquenched when several of the opposing team landed on top of him.

The party after the game was a jubilant affair, in spite of the aches and pains of some of the veterans, including David's black eye and Francesco's fiercely guarded secret of an aching knee.

'My hero,' said Alicia as the champagne circulated before the buffet supper. 'I hope the local press photographer caught your try, darling.'

'I hope so too—it will never happen again!' Francesco grinned down at her, then clapped Gareth on the shoulder. 'Thank you, captain. It was good today, no?'

'Absolutely brilliant,' said Gareth.

'*Daverro,*' agreed Francesco. 'How are you feeling, David?'

'Old,' was the bitter reply. 'These lads of yours are good, Francesco.'

'I'll just pop off and congratulate your old teammates, Francesco,' said Alicia. 'It was so good of them to come and help.'

She went on a round of the visiting rugby players, taking Megan with her in support, and there was a great deal of laughter and kissing of cheeks as they congratulated the jubilant men on their magnificent performance. Then everyone took their places for the buffet supper, even Zia Luisa, who was so delighted with the occasion she refused to go home until she'd seen the fireworks promised for later.

After supper Francesco made a graceful speech in two languages, handed over a sizeable cheque to the hospital administrator, then ushered everyone outside to watch the firework display.

'That was a wonderful try,' Alicia said in his ear, during a pause while the second round of fireworks was made ready. 'I screamed myself hoarse as you went tearing down the field. But we were very relieved when the final whistle blew and you came off the field unhurt.'

'We?' murmured Francesco, holding her closer. 'You mean you, Megan and your mother?'

'No. Baby and me,' she said into his chest, and felt it expand against her with a huge intake of breath.

'At last,' he breathed into her hair. 'I have been waiting so patiently for you to tell me.'

Alicia raised her eyes to his. 'You knew?'

He smiled, his eyes reflecting the rainbow of colours as round after round of coloured stars shot into the sky. 'I can count, *tesoro.*'

'Oh, I see.' She eyed him anxiously. 'Are you pleased—Papa?'

'Pleased?' He bent his head and kissed her quickly as

everyone's attention stayed with the display. 'I am the happiest man in the world. *Ti amo, tesoro.*'

As the last of the rockets went off, the world went silent and the sky was left to the stars. With a concerted sigh the guests turned back inside for a last glass of champagne. Alicia found her mother, had a quick word which widened Bron's eyes in delight, then did the same with Eira and Megan, and finally with Luisa and Bianca. Then she returned to Francesco.

'Care to make an announcement as you say goodnight?'

'If you allow me I would like that very much, *carissima— grazie.*' Francesco turned to face his guests, tapped on his glass, and once again thanked everyone, spectators and players, for making the event such a successful occasion. 'And now,' he added, putting his arm around his wife. 'Please raise your glasses to celebrate this special day. Much money was raised for the children's wing and the match was a personal triumph—I even scored a try my knees may never recover from! But as the crowning touch to the day Alicia has just given me the most wonderful news—by the end of the next Six Nations my wife and I will be parents!'

MILLS & BOON

and

**ENGLAND
RUGBY**

present

INTERNATIONAL
BILLIONAIRES

*From rich tycoons to royal playboys –
they're red-hot and ruthless*

Turn the page for more!

Read all about the players, the glamour,
the excitement of the game – and where to
escape when you want some romance!

A GIRL'S GUIDE TO RUGBY

Rugby isn't just thirty sweaty men getting muddy in a field for eighty minutes – although that can be quite appealing! It's played in more than a hundred countries across five continents, by all ages and sexes. It's a fun, fast and furious spectator sport – and it's also a great family day out.

International locations

Want some winter sun? Jet off to **Dubai** for the International Rugby Sevens. Or pop to **Argentina** for a spot of tango, polo *and* rugby. Or how about a trip to **Sydney** for the **Tri Nations**?

Glamorous audience

Don't forget to keep an eye out for celebrities watching the game with you! You might spot **Prince William** and **Prince Harry** at Twickenham, or **Charlotte Church** cheering for Gavin Henson at the Millennium Stadium in Cardiff. **Zara Phillips** is also dating a rugby player.

Not just for the boys

Who knows? You may be inspired to have a go yourself! Rugby is one of the best all-round **workouts**, building strength, cardiovascular fitness and toning those all-important wobbly bits. And nothing is better than being part of a winning team!

ENGLAND
RUGBY

Rugby – the basics

First time at a match? Always wondered what a line-out was? Confused by an offside call? These basic facts will get you through!

1. **Vital statistics**
   There are fifteen players on each side. Each match lasts for eighty minutes, and the team plays forty minutes in one direction and then they swap ends.

2. **Scoring**
   The object is to score more points than the opposition. Teams can score a try, penalty, drop goal or conversion.

3. **Try**
   When the ball is grounded over the try line and within the area before the dead ball line it earns five points.

4. **Conversion**
   After a team scores a try, a conversion, a free kick at goal from a point directly in line with where the try was scored, is worth two points.

5. **Drop goal**
   When, in open play, the ball is kicked between the rugby post uprights and above the crossbar, in a drop goal, it earns three points.

6. **Penalty**
   This can be awarded by the referee for infringements of the rules of rugby and if successfully kicked it earns three points.

7. **Offside**
   This is the key rule of rugby, and it's a lot simpler than football. Say your friend has the ball and she passes it to you. If she has to throw

it *back* to you, you are onside. If she throws it *forward*, you are offside. Players must be behind the ball.

8. **Tackle**

   Not as rude as it sounds! The player with the ball is brought to the ground by a tackle, and they must either pass or release the ball.

9. **Ruck**

   If a player loses possession of the ball, the team form a ruck to try to win the ball back, trying to ruck the ball back with their feet.

10. **Maul**

    If a ball carrier is held up (a tackle which doesn't bring the player to the ground) a maul may form, when players can only join the maul from behind their team-mates and not come in from the side.

11. **Line-out**

    If the ball goes out of the field of play, into touch, a line-out restarts the game. Players from both teams form parallel lines while the ball is thrown down the middle of the line-out from the touch line and players are lifted by their team-mates in an effort to win the ball.

12. **Scrum**

    If a player infringes the rules, for example by being offside, a scrum may be awarded, where the eight forwards from each team bind together and push against the opposition to win the ball, which is fed in down the centre of the tunnel.

HOW TO BE FABULOUS
AT THE RUGBY...

Follow our simple guide to rugby style and you'll soon have a whole new perspective on the game.

- The atmosphere before any big game is part of the fun. Make sure you get there early. And starting the match-day party with a champagne picnic means it won't really matter if you know the rules or not!

- While you want to look gorgeous, you also want to be warm. Invest in a striking full-length coat and matching scarf and gloves.

- It's chilly in the stands and the weather can never be trusted – make sure your make-up is weatherproof.

- Indulge the trend for girly wellingtons or pretty ballet shoes, as sky-scraper heels may start to pinch. Especially if your team is winning and you're leaping up and down enthusiastically!

- Be ready to join in – sing as loud as you can in support of your team, cheer on the tries and allow yourself to get into the spirit of it all. You'll be surprised at how much fun you have!

- Not sure whether you'll enjoy the game? Check out Rugby Sevens. Group tournaments are played all around the UK throughout the year, and with only seven men in each team.

- Rugby supporters are a jolly bunch. There are many new friends to be had over a beer and a hog roast!

- A rugby game is only eighty minutes long. Why stop the afternoon there? Plan a fabulous after party and play perfect hostess.

ROMANTIC RUGBY

What better excuse than the six countries of the Six Nations to treat yourself and your partner to a romantic weekend away? You can share the fun of a match, and then enjoy a new city together.

In *The Italian Count's Defiant Bride*, PR girl Alicia has her heart broken in Florence – and gets a second chance with her husband in Cardiff! The Millennium Stadium is an amazing venue for some great rugby – and after the game, take some time to explore historic Cardiff!

In the heart of Cardiff is Cardiff Castle, a site with a history that spans two thousand years. Its gothic fairytale towers and opulent interiors rich with murals, stained glass and marble are breathtaking – and each room has its own special theme, including Mediterranean gardens and Arabian decoration.

A short, scenic walk through Bute Park and the Victorian conservation area brings you to the city centre filled with shops and places to eat or drink. The exciting new Cardiff Bay development is also close at hand.

As well as all this there is Castell Coch, a fairytale castle nestling in the woods on the outskirts of the city. Its round towers and red turrets are reminiscent of castles along the bank of the river Rhine.

DID YOU KNOW

That the wives and girlfriends of rugby players are called Scrummies? Felicia Field-Hall is dating England Rugby player James Haskell – so she knows all about romance and rugby! We caught up with the glamorous model and presenter to ask her a few questions.

In your opinion, what's the difference between a Scrummie and a WAG?

Scrummie is a fairly new press title for the other halves of rugby players. Aside from pointing out the obvious, I like to think that the difference in salaries keeps us grounded! We are all very much career-focused girls. I think this probably benefits the boys in the sense that anyone who dates a professional sportsman will know that their sport is all-consuming. I think it's a nice escape for them to talk about what we do during the day!

How do you manage to combine romance and rugby?

As you can imagine, self-discipline and dedication are foremost to any rugby player. I'll admit that it's often hard to break their focus away from the game, but I think, like any career where you are expected to put in the extra mile with everything you do if you want to succeed, you have to find those small moments to share. It can be anything from a posh dinner to simply walking the dog.

Which do you think is the most romantic of the cities in which the Six Nations are played? Why?

By far and away, Rome. Last year was my first visit to Rome, and everything from the fabulous hotel in which the team stayed to the brilliant atmosphere of the Stadio Flaminio makes it the perfect setting for any Mills & Boon novel.

Any tips for looking your best at a wet and windy Twickenham watching the rugby?

This is, almost certainly, the hardest look to achieve. Buy a protective "shield" in the form of a hooded coat. Equally important, I have found out the hard way, is to have a back-up black-tie dress tucked away, in case you are asked to the post-match dinner.

Have you ever been tempted to enter the scrum and play yourself?

Absolutely not! Although both myself and the girlfriend of an England winger once shared a very similar dream that we both had to take the place of our other halves on the bench. In this dream you would have thought we'd both be terrified, but no, in both separate dreams we went on to score winning tries for England, no small feat for myself playing number six at the time.

What's your ideal romantic getaway?

I love extremes, from The Grosvenor House Hotel in Dubai, where one can happily tuck into oysters for breakfast, to a pint of cider in a Cotswolds cottage hotel with the dog. You don't always have to get on a plane to find somewhere special.

What's the most romantic thing you've ever done?

I think it's the lots of little things that count. From surprising someone at an airport to making heart-shaped cookies, it's all about spontaneity and doing something to show that you know your other half's likes and dislikes.

Coming next month from

MILLS & BOON®

and

**ENGLAND
RUGBY**

*a proud, arrogant sheikh will come
face to face with his past!*

The Sheikh's Love-Child

by

Kate Hewitt

Read on for a sneak preview…

Lucy Banks craned her head to catch a glimpse of the island of Biryal as the plane burst from a thick blanket of cottony clouds and the Indian Ocean stretched below them, an endless expanse of glittering blue.

She squinted, looking for a strip of land, anything green, to signal that they were approaching their destination, but there was nothing to be seen.

Breathing a sigh of relief, she leaned back in her seat. She wasn't ready to face Biryal or, more to the point, its crown prince, Sheikh Khaled el Farrar.

Khaled…just his name brought a tumbled kaleidoscope of memories and images to her mind – his easy smile, the way his darkly golden eyes had caught and held hers across a crowded pub after a match, the fizz of feeling that one look caused within her, bubbles of anticipation racing along her veins, buoying her heart.

And then, unbidden, came the stronger,

sweeter, and more sensual memories. The ones she'd kept close to her heart even as she tried to keep them from her mind. Now, for a moment, she indulged them, indulged herself, and let the memories wash over her, making her blush in shame even as her heart ached with longing. Still.

Lying in Khaled's arms, late afternoon sunlight pouring through the window, and laughter – pure joy – rising unheeded within her. His lips on hers, his hands smoothing her skin, touching her like a treasure, as their bodies moved, their hearts joined…and she'd been utterly shameless.

Shamelessly she'd revelled in his attention, his caress. She'd delighted in the freedom of loving and being loved. It had seemed so simple, so obvious, so *right*.

The shame had come later, scalding her soul and breaking her heart when Khaled had left England – left her – without an explanation or even a goodbye.

She'd faced his teammates, who'd watched her fall hard, seen Khaled reel her in with practised ease, and now knew he'd just walked away.

Lucy swallowed and forced the memories back. Even the sweet, secret ones hurt, scars that had never healed, just scabbed over till she helplessly picked at them once more.

"All right?" Eric Chandler slid into the seat next to her, his eyebrows lifting in compassionate query.

Lucy tilted her chin at a determined angle and forced a smile. "I'm fine."

Of all the people who had witnessed her infatuation with Khaled, Eric perhaps understood it – her – the best. He'd been Khaled's best friend, and when Khaled had gone, he'd become one of hers. But she didn't want his compassion; it was too close to pity.

"You didn't have to come," he said, and Lucy heard the faint thread of bitterness in his voice. This was a conversation they'd had before, when the opportunity of a friendly match with Biryal's fledgling team had come up.

She shook her head wearily, not wanting to go over old ground. Eric knew why she'd come as much as she did. "You don't owe him anything," Eric continued, and Lucy sighed. She suspected Eric had felt as betrayed as she had when Khaled had left so abruptly, even though he never said as much.

"I owe Khaled the truth," she replied quietly. Her fingers flicked nervously at the metal clasp of her seat belt. "I owe him that much, at least."

The truth, and that was all. A message given and received, and then she could walk away with a clear conscience, a light heart. Or so she hoped. Needed. She'd come to Biryal for that, craved the closure she hoped seeing Khaled face to face would finally bring.

Khaled el Farrar had made a fool of her once. He would not do so again.

INTERNATIONAL BILLIONAIRES

WIN A LUXURY WEEKEND IN LONDON!

We've got a luxury weekend stay at the Home of England Rugby up for grabs in every edition of the International Billionaires mini-series(x 8).

You and a partner will be treated to two nights' accommodation in the brand-new London Marriott Hotel Twickenham, where you'll receive a free tour of the famous stadium, as well as entry to the World Rugby Museum.

TWICKENHAM
WORLD RUGBY MUSEUM
& STADIUM TOURS

Marriott.
LONDON TWICKENHAM

You'll also each come away with a free goody bag, packed with books, England Rugby clothing and other accessories.

INTERNATIONAL · BILLIONAIRES

To enter, complete the entry form below and send to:
Mills & Boon RFU/May Prize Draw,
Eton House, 18–24 Paradise Road,
Richmond, Surrey, TW9 1SR

Mills & Boon® Rugby Prize Draw (June)

Name: _____

Address: _____

Post Code:_____

Daytime Telephone No: _____

E-mail Address: _____

❑ I have read the terms and conditions (please tick this box before entering).

❑ Please tick here if you do not wish to receive special offers from
Harlequin Mills & Boon Ltd.

Closing date for entries is 19th July 2009

Terms & Conditions

1. Draw open to UK and Eire residents aged 18 and over. No purchase necessary. One entry per household per prize draw only. 2. Prizes are non-transferable and no cash alternatives will be offered. 3. All travel expenses to and from Twickenham must be covered by the prize winner. 4. All prizes are subject to availability. Should any prize be unavailable, a prize of similar value will be substituted. 5. Employees and immediate family members of Harlequin Mills & Boon Ltd are not eligible to enter. 6. Prize winners will be randomly selected from the eligible entries received. No correspondence will be entered into and no entry returned. 7. To be eligible, all entries must be received by 19th July 2009. 8. Prize-winner notification will be made by e-mail or letter no later than 15 days after the deadline for entry. 9. No responsibility can be accepted for entries that are lost, delayed or damaged. Proof of postage cannot be accepted as proof of delivery. 10. If any winner notification or prize is returned as undeliverable, an alternative winner will be drawn from eligible entries. 11. Names of competition winners are available on request.

MILLS & BOON

MODERN

On sale 3rd July 2009

RUTHLESSLY BEDDED, FORCIBLY WEDDED
by Abby Green

Ruthless millionaire Vincenzo seduced Ellie and cruelly
discarded her. But she's now pregnant! The Italian will claim
her again…as his bride!

THE DESERT KING'S BEJEWELLED BRIDE
by Sabrina Philips

Kaliq Al-Zahir A'zam was outraged when Tamara Weston
rejected his marriage proposal. Now Tamara will model his royal
jewels – and deliver to him the wedding night he was denied…

BOUGHT: FOR HIS CONVENIENCE OR PLEASURE?
by Maggie Cox

Needing a mother for his orphaned nephew, magnate Nikolai
tracks Ellie down to make her his unwillingly wedded wife!

THE PLAYBOY OF PENGARROTH HALL
by Susanne James

Fleur would never make a one-night mistress – but she could
be the mistress of Pengarroth Hall – if only Sebastian
can overcome his allergy to marriage…

THE SANTORINI MARRIAGE BARGAIN
by Margaret Mayo

Zarek Diakos has decided Rhianne's wasted as his secretary.
He's in need of a bride: under the warm Santorini sun he'll
show Rhianne it's a position she can't refuse!

Now back in print from Titan Books

STAR TREK®
ENEMY UNSEEN
by V.E. Mitchell

Transporting a diplomatic party is nothing new for
Captain James T. Kirk and the crew of the *Enterprise* -
but this particular mission promises trouble from
the start.

For one thing, the wife of the Federation ambassador
on this trip is an old flame of Kirk's - and she's
determined to see they resume their romance where
they left off. Of course, when another ambassador
presents Kirk with three of his wives, finding time for
the first romance, let alone any of his other duties, is
going to prove nearly impossible.

When a diplomatic attache is murdered, and the prime
suspect is one of his crew members, Kirk begins to
wish that Starfleet Command would consider using
some other Starship to ferry diplomatic personnel...

For a complete list of Star Trek publications, T-shirts and badges please send a large SAE to Titan Books Mail Order, 19 Valentine Place, London, SE1 8QH. Please quote reference ST55.